Emily Sneller

Elizabeth Gail and Double Trouble

Hilda Stahl

Tyndale House Publishers, Inc., Wheaton, Illinois

Dedicated with love to
Jeff, Ann, and Jeffrey Arnett

The Elizabeth Gail Series

Cover and interior illustration by Kathy Kulin

Library of Congress Catalog Card Number 88-51708
ISBN 0-8423-0801-6
Copyright 1982 by Hilda Stahl
All rights reserved
Printed in the United States of America

95   94   93   92   91
10   9   8   7   6   5   4   3

Contents

ONE
A strange call

The phone rang and Libby turned from the piano and laughed aloud. It had to be someone else calling to say he or she could come to the birthday party. It rang again and Libby hurried to answer it. She almost knocked over the desk calendar on Vera's small desk.

"Hello." Libby waltzed around the desk, her hazel eyes sparkling.

"Libby?"

She stopped short, her breath caught in her throat. The whisper at the other end sent chills running up and down her spine. She clutched the phone tighter. "This is Libby."

"I have to see you and talk to you."

"Who is this?" Libby wanted to slam down the receiver but she couldn't move. Her mouth felt cotton-dry. Was it Mother? Oh, it couldn't be!

"I need your help, Libby." The whisper was frantic, but it was suddenly cut off, leaving only a loud buzz.

Libby dropped the receiver in place with a clatter, then locked her icy fingers together. She sank into

Vera's chair and tried to think. What should she do? The person had sounded desperate! Libby looked helplessly around the room. Her eyes met Ben's. He was looking at her questioningly, the book on chess hanging limply in his hand.

"What's wrong, Elizabeth?"

She opened her mouth, then closed it, and swallowed hard.

"Was it a prank call?" asked Ben sharply as he rushed to stand beside her. "Maybe it was someone's idea of a joke. Maybe someone you didn't invite to your thirteenth birthday party wanted to come, so they called to scare you."

Libby shivered. "The person needed my help," she whispered. "Isn't that strange? Who could I help? I'm the one who always needs help!"

Ben shook his head. His red hair was mussed. He tugged his black sweatshirt over his jeans. "We can't do anything about it now. Come play chess with me and get your mind off the call."

"Do you think it was Mother?" whispered Libby, her eyes wide.

"Your mother hasn't bothered you for a long time, Elizabeth. She signed the paper saying we could adopt you, didn't she?"

Libby nodded. It had taken Mother a long time to agree to let the Johnson family adopt her, but she had signed. Soon the Johnsons would adopt her and she'd be Elizabeth Gail Johnson instead of Libby Dobbs.

"Forget the phone call, Elizabeth." Ben stood with his hands on his hips. "Play chess with me."

"Oh, Ben, you know I can't remember the moves." She pushed herself up and took a deep breath. "Go back

8

to your book. I'll be all right." Would there ever be a time in her life when she wouldn't be afraid?

Ben motioned to the piano. "Sit down and play for a while. That always relaxes you."

She grinned and shrugged. Ben was right. "But if the phone rings again, you answer it, Ben."

"I will." He picked up his book, then sat cross-legged on the carpet with his back against the end of the couch.

A fire crackled in the fireplace. Snow blew against the windows and Libby was glad she was inside where it was warm.

She picked out a lesson book as she forced her mind off the scary phone call. Why should she be afraid? She was no longer an unloved aid kid who was kicked from one terrible family to another. The Johnsons had prayed her into their family. They loved her and she loved them. They didn't care that she was tall and thin and ugly. They really loved her. A warmth spread through her and she was able to smile.

Libby brushed her brown hair away from her face, then wrinkled her nose as she remembered how she'd looked when she'd first come to the Johnson farm. Miss Miller had driven her away from the city, saying she'd like living in the country with the Johnsons. She'd been dressed in an ugly brown dress much too large for her and her hair was in two skinny braids. Vera had cut her hair, washed it, and blown it dry, and Libby had looked in the mirror and thought she was almost pretty. But she'd never be pretty like short, dainty Susan with her red-gold hair. Ben and Kevin and Susan were born into the Johnson family. Toby was already adopted and Libby knew she soon would be, too.

She touched the piano keys, wishing she could play as

well as Vera. Someday she would. Vera often said so.

Someone touched her arm and she jumped, then looked back to see Chuck and Vera smiling at her.

"Who was on the phone a while ago?" asked Vera, standing with her blonde head against Chuck's arm.

Libby swallowed hard as she slipped off the bench and stood up. She was almost as tall as Vera. "I don't know, Mom." Libby's hands shook and she quickly locked them together behind her. "Someone asked me for help, and I don't know who it was."

Chuck caught her cold hand in his and held it. His hair was a little darker red than Ben's with just a touch of gray at the temples. "Maybe someone was playing a joke on you. All your friends know about your thirteenth birthday party Friday night. Someone might have called to say he was coming, then did that to you."

"It certainly isn't funny," said Vera sharply, and Ben agreed.

"We have nothing to fear," said Chuck as he walked to the couch and sat down. He pulled Vera down on one side of him and Libby on the other. "We won't let a phone call upset the fun we're having getting ready for your birthday, Elizabeth."

"That's right!" said Vera with a firm nod. "Ten boys and girls have already called to say they'll come. If this cold weather keeps up, we'll be able to ice skate for sure. And we'll decorate the heart-shaped cakes and fix up the basement."

Chuck rubbed his cheek on Libby's hair. "You'll be a real Valentine's sweetheart on your birthday. I'm glad you don't mind being teased about your birthday being February 14."

Libby rolled her eyes. "A lot of things used to bother

10

me, but don't now. I think Kevin is glad. He sure got in a lot of trouble when he teased me." She laughed and shrugged her shoulders. "I got in a lot of trouble, too."

"We're all learning and growing," said Chuck. "We're learning more and more to be like Jesus."

Libby nodded thankfully.

Just then the phone rang. Libby jumped, her eyes wide in alarm.

"It's all right, Elizabeth," said Chuck, patting her shoulder. "I'll answer it."

Vera moved close to Libby and slipped her arms around her. Libby leaned against Vera as she watched Chuck talking. He hung up and turned with a smile.

"April and May Brakie said they'll be here for your party, Elizabeth."

Libby sighed in relief, then grinned sheepishly.

"I'm glad the twins are coming," said Vera. "It's been a long time since I've seen them."

"It's going to be a fun party," said Ben.

Libby nodded. Was she going to let one strange phone call ruin her life? No! She was not! A shiver ran down her spine and she held Vera's hand tighter.

TWO
Baby-sitting with Amy

Libby frowned at the noise on the school bus. How could she and Jill carry on a conversation with all this racket? Why didn't Mrs. Hooper just turn around and yell for everyone to sit down and be quiet? Libby saw Ben tell Toby to be quiet, and she knew he was reminding Toby that he didn't want to get into more trouble. Kevin sat talking quietly with Paul Noteboom. Maybe Toby had wanted to sit with them but they wouldn't let him. Sometimes he acted like such a big baby instead of practically ten years old. He probably still sucked his thumb when nobody was looking.

Just then he turned and when he saw her watching him, he made a face. His face was dirty, blotting out some of the freckles and his red hair stood on end with electricity from his hat. Finally he turned around and slumped down in his seat. Libby felt like slapping his face, then shrugged. Let him act dumb. She wasn't his mother.

Libby turned her head to whisper to Jill, then closed her mouth. Jill was looking at Adam Feuder the same way Susan looked at Joe Wilkens! How could Jill do that? She'd said over and over that she didn't have time for boys, that she was going to be a famous writer. She'd said she and Libby could be best friends since neither one liked boys and both were going to be famous someday.

With a frown Libby jabbed Jill's arm. Jill looked around sharply.

"Did you say something, Libby?"

Libby nodded. Some day she'd convince Jill Noteboom to call her Elizabeth. "I've been trying to tell you about the strange phone call I got yesterday afternoon."

Jill slid down low in her seat so her ear was close to Libby's mouth. "Tell me. This should be very good for me to listen to. I might be able to use it in my book."

Libby told her how the person had said she needed her help. "I think it was a girl, but it could've been a boy."

"Maybe this girl is being held captive and got to a phone just long enough to call you."

Libby shook her head. "That's crazy. This isn't a TV show!"

"But with your past, you know a lot of girls who could be in serious trouble."

Libby flushed. She'd finally told Jill about the people she'd known while she still lived with Mother, and about the people she'd met while she lived at foster homes where no one loved her.

The bus stopped at a railroad crossing and everyone sat quietly. The brakes hissed and Mrs. Hooper drove across the tracks, then turned left. Jill suggested others who could've called, but Libby shook her head.

With a sigh Libby leaned her head back and tried to place the voice of the caller. It had seemed very familiar.

How could that be? Whispered voices sounded a lot alike. Why think about it? She should be thinking of her thirteenth birthday party instead of the phone call. Maybe Jill would want to help decorate the cakes and the basement.

Libby turned to Jill only to find Jill once again staring at Adam Feuder.

"He'd never like me for a girlfriend," Jill said sadly in a low voice. "I'm too big for him. Once he grows more, he'll be taller than I." She sighed and folded her arms. "Unless I grow even more. I might be the only woman giant in the entire school."

"Mom says that tall girls can be very beautiful."

Jill shook her head and her brown eyes were full of sadness. "But not tall, fat girls! My hair is a disaster and my body is terrible and no boy will ever look twice at me unless he has to look twice just to see all of me."

"Oh, Jill." Libby wanted to say something to cheer Jill up, but she didn't know what to say.

Finally the bus stopped and Jill stood up to get off. She said good-bye to Libby and walked toward the open door. Libby felt the cold air rush into the warm bus. Someone threw a paper wad and it hit Jill on the back. She just kept walking and Libby knew Jill was embarrassed. Libby glanced at Adam to find him watching Jill and Paul step off the bus. Did Adam know that Jill loved him? He was always so busy playing chess with Ben that he wouldn't notice anything. Maybe she should have a talk with Adam. But what could she say? "Adam, Jill loves you. She wants you to be her boyfriend." Oh, she couldn't do that! But Susan would if she knew.

Libby looked across the aisle where Susan sat holding

hands with Joe Wilkens. Susan's face glowed and her red-gold hair seemed alive. As the bus stopped again Susan reluctantly pulled her hand free and stood up. Libby walked quickly down the aisle, knowing Susan was right behind her, wishing she could ride down the road to Joe's house.

"Race you!" shouted Toby, running fast down the long drive. Kevin and Ben followed him just as Goosy Poosy ran toward them, honking noisily.

Libby lifted her face to the chilly wind and let it blow her hair back. She would always live on the Johnson farm even when she became a famous concert pianist!

Rex barked and pushed his nose against her hand. She knelt beside him and hugged him tightly. "I love you, Rex. I love you as much as I love Snowball." Rex licked her face and she laughed.

"I have to go change and do chores, Rex. I'll be outside later." Libby hugged him again, then ran to the back door, catching the storm door before it closed after Susan.

Just as Libby hung her jacket beside Vera's farm coat, Vera walked onto the back porch. Smells of fresh baked bread made Libby's mouth water. She could eat a whole loaf herself.

"Susan and Libby, I told Lisa Parr that you'd baby-sit with Amy for a couple of hours," said Vera with a smile. She was dressed in blue jeans and vest with a long-sleeved red blouse. "The boys will do your chores."

"I haven't seen baby Amy for a long time," said Libby, laughing. "I'll love baby-sitting with her."

Susan shook her head. "I won't! Joe's coming over in an hour and we're going to play Ping-Pong."

"No, Susan." Vera stood with her hands on her waist.

"I told you that Joe can come over one day a week, and he's coming Friday night for Libby's birthday. He cannot come today!"

Tears filled Susan's eyes and ran down her cheeks. "I want him to come today! We've already made plans!"

"Put your coat on right now, Susan. You and Libby are going to the Parrs'. Lisa said she'd have a snack for you." Vera lifted Susan's jacket off the hook and handed it to her. Susan's face was dark with anger as she jerked the jacket away from Vera and slipped it on.

"I could go alone," said Libby in a small, tight voice as she clutched her jacket. Fighting made her think of Mother, and she didn't want to!

Vera shook her head and her blonde hair swished prettily. "I'm sure you could handle it, but I'd feel much better with both of you there."

Later in the car Libby peeked at Susan's scowling face, then looked back at the road. She would not let Susan ruin their fun time with baby Amy!

"Brian said he'd bring you home," said Vera as she pulled into the drive. "If you need me for anything, just call and I'll be right down."

Libby stood beside the car as Susan begged to go home. Vera was firm about Susan baby-sitting, so she jumped out and slammed the door. Libby knew that if Susan didn't behave she'd end up in the study having a very serious talk with Chuck. Libby twisted her boot in the snow as she remembered the many times she'd had to talk with him.

The door opened and Lisa called for them to come right in. Lisa's brown hair hung almost to her waist and her blue eyes sparkled with excitement. "Brian and I have saved for three weeks and we finally have enough money to go out for dinner. We won't be gone too long. Amy has already eaten, but she might want a cookie later."

Amy toddled to Libby and lifted her arms. Libby laughed and picked her up. She smelled like graham crackers.

"Hi, girls." Brian walked from the tiny bedroom into the tiny living room. His hair was still damp from his shower. "Lisa baked cookies for you. There's milk and Kool-Aid in the refrigerator to drink." He helped Lisa on with her coat and said they'd be on their way.

"You know where everything is," said Lisa as she lifted her long hair out of her coat collar and let it cascade around her small body. "Thanks, girls. You've helped make this a special night."

Brian grinned as he opened the door for Lisa. "It's our second anniversary. Last year we couldn't go out at all." He lifted his hand, said good-bye to the girls, and closed the door behind them.

Susan plopped down on the couch and folded her arms. "I'm going to get married when I'm seventeen just like Lisa did. And I'm going to marry Joe Wilkens and Mom can't stop me!"

Libby sat on a chair with Amy on her lap. Amy tugged at Libby's nose and Libby pulled her hand away. "Susan, you'll fall in love a lot of times before you're old enough to get married."

"I will not! I am going to marry Joe. Maybe we'll get married when I'm sixteen! That's only three more years."

"More than three, Susan. You won't be thirteen until April 25."

Susan jumped up, her fists doubled at her sides. "You

think you're so big because you're going to be thirteen Friday!"

Before Libby could answer, Amy stood up in her lap and said insistently, "Cookie!" She looked so cute that both Libby and Susan began to laugh. Once they started to laugh, they couldn't stop. They had only to look at each other to start all over again. Oh, it felt good to laugh instead of being angry! They laughed until their faces were red and tears were streaming down their cheeks. All the while, Amy stood up, swinging back and forth on Libby's hands and shouting, "Cookie!" and laughing with them.

Finally, Libby and Susan got themselves under control and took Amy to the kitchen to get her a cookie. They got cookies and milk for themselves, too. When they got back to the living room, Libby looked at Amy sitting on the floor. Had Mother ever held her and laughed with her? Had she ever baked cookies for Libby? All Libby could remember was being beaten and starved and yelled at. Once she was adopted, Libby knew that she would never see her mother again. How would Mother feel? Was it right for Libby to be so glad that she would never see her own mother again?

Resolutely, Libby put those thoughts out of her mind. She wouldn't think about Mother! It still hurt too much.

THREE
February 13

Libby pulled her red and pink bedspread in place, then turned to brush her hair. Tomorrow she would be thirteen years old! She leaned toward the mirror. Did she look any older? Her pointed chin, straight nose, and short brown hair looked just the same. Would she stay ugly all her life? She pictured the large audience of people watching her as she performed on the piano. They would say, "My, Elizabeth Gail Johnson certainly can play, but isn't she ugly?"

Elizabeth Gail Johnson! Libby's heart raced as she realized that soon she'd be adopted. Chuck had said it wouldn't be much longer. Libby didn't like waiting for the judge's calendar to be free enough to take them. Twice he'd had to postpone their meeting.

Toby was shouting that it was time for the bus as Libby ran downstairs. The grandfather clock ticked loudly, striking once to say it was seven-thirty. The phone rang and Vera called that it was for Libby. She answered it in the family room. It had to be Jill asking her to bring the markers that she needed for math.

Libby said hello, then waited. She could hear breathing and she said hello louder. There was a click, then a buzz. Whoever it was had hung up. Libby frowned as she replaced the receiver. Her heart was pounding. Was it the same caller who had called Sunday?

"Hurry, Libby," called Susan. "Time to pray and go outside."

Libby licked her dry lips as she rushed to the back porch for her jacket. She slipped it on, then picked up her books.

"Who was on the phone?" asked Vera as she turned Toby's collar up. She tied his scarf, then glanced at Libby with her eyebrows raised.

"I don't know. Whoever it was hung up."

Vera frowned, then smiled. "Oh, maybe it was someone who saw the bus coming." She looked around as she fixed Kevin's collar. Then she said, "Let's pray now before you go."

Libby bowed her head as Vera thanked the Lord for his love, protection, and help.

Kevin and Toby rushed out the door, fighting over who was to be first on the bus. Vera caught Libby in a close hug.

"Tomorrow is your birthday, honey. It'll be one of the best days of your life. Thirteen is a very special age."

Libby kissed Vera's cheek and smelled her cologne. Vera always smelled good. Mother had always smelled like stale tobacco and beer. Libby pushed the thought aside as she hurried out the door into the cold day. Rex barked from his doghouse and Libby called to him, "See you tonight, Rex."

She lifted her head. She could hear the roar of the bus coming closer, so she ran fast down the long driveway.

Snow covered the large lawn. A snowman stood next to the tree with the swing hanging from it. Libby's hands had practically frozen when she'd helped Toby build the snowman one day while Kevin was playing with Paul.

On the bus Libby waited impatiently for Jill to get on, but when she did she was so busy talking about the chapter she'd written in her book that Libby couldn't tell her about the phone call.

As they stepped off the bus and walked toward the school, Jill said in a low voice, "Did Adam say if he's going to your party or not?"

Libby sighed impatiently. Why didn't Jill keep her mind on her writing? "He's coming, Jill."

Jill flushed with pleasure. "I wonder if Dad could offer to pick him up since we drive right past his place when we go to yours."

"Why don't you just ask Adam? Don't be afraid to talk to him."

Just then someone shouted at Libby and she turned to find April and May Brakie running toward her. Both girls were dressed in dark blue skirts and white ski jackets. April wore a red hat and scarf and May wore green.

"We can't wait for your party, Libby!" April squeezed Libby's arm and laughed, then turned to Jill. "Hi, Jill."

"Hi." Jill smiled and looked from one twin to the other. Libby knew Jill was trying to decide who was who.

"Did you invite Joanne Tripper?" whispered May with a giggle.

"No! She wouldn't come if I did." Libby stepped aside to let several boys and girls pass. "I hear that she takes piano lessons from Mrs. Mayhew now. Maybe Joanne will leave me alone."

"She really was determined to get Rachael Avery to drop you so she could take from her," said April. "I guess if I was as good at piano as Joanne is, I'd want to take from the best teacher, too."

Libby nodded. Once she'd been jealous of Joanne's ability, but the Lord had helped her get rid of her jealousy.

Inside the school Libby hung her jacket in her locker, then turned and almost bumped into Dave Boomer who was standing awkwardly waiting to talk to her.

His face turned very red. "Mom said to tell you that I'll be at your party tomorrow. I was supposed to call last night but I forgot."

Libby smiled. "That's all right. Be sure to bring your ice skates. Ben's going to build a bonfire next to the pond." Libby felt like shouting. Could it be true that plain Libby Dobbs was having this grand birthday party? Never in her life had anyone given her a party like this!

She walked to class with her head high. She was not an aid kid any longer! Suddenly someone bumped against her and she staggered, then caught herself on the drinking fountain before she fell. She heard a giggle and knew that it was Joanne Tripper and that she'd pushed her on purpose.

"I heard about your dumb birthday party tomorrow," said Joanne, flipping her long blonde hair back. She was dressed in a dusty rose dress that fit snug in just the right places. Joanne always dressed to show off her figure.

Libby tugged her sweater over her dark green slacks. She was as tall as Joanne, but as thin as a stringbean. "I'm going to be late to class." She tried to walk away, but Joanne caught her arm in a tight grip. "Let me go," Libby said through her teeth.

"I've had plenty of big birthday parties! Probably a lot bigger than yours will be."

"Good for you!"

"You think you're hot stuff, don't you?" Joanne's blue eyes narrowed and she leaned close to Libby. "Well, you're not! You have a big surprise coming that will make you remember that you're only a no-good aid kid."

Libby jerked hard and broke Joanne's grip. "Big talk! You can't scare me, Joanne Tripper!" What could she mean? What did Joanne know that she wasn't telling yet?

"Just wait till you learn what Marie Dobbs is going to do at your party tomorrow."

Libby's legs almost buckled under her, but she forced them to hold her up. What was Mother's plan this time? "You don't know what you're talking about, Joanne."

She lifted her head and her long blonde hair fell almost to her narrow waist. "You'll see tomorrow."

Libby wanted to grab Joanne and shake the information out of her. She knew Joanne wanted her to do something like that, so she lifted her pointed chin and walked to her first class. She sank into her seat and trembled. Was Joanne bluffing, or would Mother show up at the party?

A paper hit Libby's arm, then dropped to the floor. Who was throwing a note to her? She glanced quickly around, but everyone was looking at the page the teacher had called.

Carefully Libby picked up the note and slowly opened it. Her eyes focused on the words just as Mr. Pasculli's hand covered the paper and her hand. She wanted to slide under her seat and disappear in a puff of dust.

"Notes so early, Libby?" He kept the note but

dropped her hand. "I would think that this class has learned not to pass notes. This is the final warning."

"I didn't pass a note," said Libby in a low, tight voice.

"In my class the passee is as guilty as the passer."

Libby's face flamed at the giggles. Once she would have leaped up and sworn at Mr. Pasculli and the class, but now that she was a Christian, she wouldn't. She glanced at the teacher, then back at the pencil clutched in her hand.

"The note says, 'Marie Dobbs is your real mother.' Libby, is Marie Dobbs your mother?" Libby knew he was only trying to embarrass her.

She hesitated, then nodded. How many kids knew Marie Dobbs? It would be terrible if anyone knew what she was like! Joanne knew. Had Joanne flipped the note to her?

Mr. Pasculli crumpled the note and dropped it in the wastebasket. "Back to science. We've wasted enough time on Libby and her note."

Libby glanced at Joanne to find her smirking with satisfaction. She *had* written the note! Libby's eyes narrowed. How could she learn Mother's plan from Joanne? Was there a plan? Was Joanne doing this to make more trouble?

Libby looked unseeingly at her science book as she wished that she and Joanne were alone in the room. If she had five minutes alone with Joanne, she could make her talk fast!

FOUR
Happy thirteenth, Libby

Libby looped her narrow red belt through her red cords,
then tugged her soft white sweater down. She looked
like a valentine with the red heart-shaped barrettes
holding her hair back from her face. Oh, today she was
thirteen years old! In just a few minutes the pond would
be full of skaters who were celebrating her birthday
with her. Her stomach tightened painfully. Would
Mother show up and embarrass her? She shook her
head. Chuck had said that he'd make sure she didn't.
He'd said that Joanne had just been trying to upset her.
They'd all prayed for the birthday party to be fun
without any trouble, and it would be! It had to be!

Libby turned to her desk to read the birthday card
from Grandma and Grandpa Johnson. She smiled as
she remembered the fun she'd had with them at their
home. She would not think about the scare she'd had
when she'd met Phyllis LaDere and Tammy. Her aunt
had looked like Mother and Libby hadn't wanted to get
acquainted. Where was her cousin now? She hadn't
liked the kind of life her mother was living.

Libby picked up the shiny puzzle box that her real dad had sent her for her twelfth birthday and rubbed her hand across it. It had taken a long time to open it and find the secrets inside. Her real dad was dead and Chuck was the only dad she wanted or needed. Soon Chuck and Vera would be her parents, not just foster parents. Libby smiled and set the puzzle box beside the birthday cards. Uncle Luke and Aunt Gwen had sent a card with ten dollars in it. Scottie had painstakingly printed his name at the bottom of the card and Libby laughed in delight. She had wanted them at her special birthday party, but they'd said they couldn't come. Uncle Luke had said that he'd remember that he owed her a birthday spanking, plus a pinch to grow an inch.

With her chin high Libby walked from her room, then downstairs to join the others. It had been fun decorating the cakes and the basement. After skating everyone was coming inside to eat and watch her open her gifts. She smiled with excitement. She couldn't wait to see the gifts! She thought of all the years when she hadn't gotten anything, not even a cake with candles, and for a minute she felt sad. But she wouldn't think about that now.

The phone rang as she walked past the family room and she jumped, her fingers twining nervously in her brown hair. Susan answered and stopped Libby, holding the phone to her.

Reluctantly Libby answered, her hands feeling damp with perspiration.

"Happy birthday, Elizabeth."

"Grandpa! Grandma!" Libby turned to Susan, her eyes sparkling. "It's Grandma and Grandpa Johnson! They said 'Happy Birthday' to me!"

"Talk to them, Libby," said Susan with a laugh and a nudge. "You can talk to me later."

Libby leaned against Vera's desk. "I got your card."

As they talked, she could picture Grandma on the kitchen extension and Grandpa on the bedroom extension. They said they'd try to visit some weekend soon and that they'd seen Ruth LaDere.

"How is she? I wrote her another letter last week. She's written five times to me so far!" Libby laughed as she thought of her real grandma and Grandma's big cat Albert. Maybe someday Grandma LaDere would accept her love and attention. Her letters had been very short and almost unfriendly.

"You have a wonderful birthday, Elizabeth," said Grandpa.

"I wish we were there," said Grandma. "Have fun, honey."

Libby talked a while longer, then reluctantly hung up, tears filling her eyes. She wanted them to be here right now to enjoy her party with her.

"Let's go out, Libby," said Vera as she walked into the family room. "Ben said the guests are driving in." Vera slipped her arm around Libby's waist and walked with her to the back porch.

Libby reached for her snowmobile suit, then stopped, her hand in mid-air. Hanging on her hook was a red and white jacket with red ski pants. She looked questioningly at Vera and Vera laughed.

"Happy birthday, sweetheart. And happy Valentine's Day."

Libby hesitated, then hugged Vera tightly. "Thank you! Thank you, Mom! I love them!"

"I'm glad." Vera kissed Libby's cheek, then stepped back as Libby pulled on the ski pants and jacket. Oh, but they were warm and snug! She felt beautiful all at once. She spun around and laughed, then stopped as Susan walked toward her.

"I have something for you, Libby." Susan stood with her hands behind her back and an excited look on her face.

"What is it, Susan?" Libby could barely stand still.

Slowly Susan held out her hands. In one hand was a red and white ski cap with a matching scarf. Inside the cap nestled red gloves.

"Oh, Susan! Oh!" Libby pulled on the cap and wrapped the scarf around her neck. It was perfect with her jacket and pants. The gloves warmed her hands instantly. She wanted to say many things, but her throat closed up and she couldn't speak.

Outdoors, the chilly wind couldn't penetrate her new jacket and pants. Libby dashed to the pond where she heard shouts and laughter. This was her day! She felt very, very special!

Several boys and girls shouted hello and waved. Jill ran to Libby's side, crying. "Oh, Libby! I love your outfit! You look fantastic! I could use you in one of my books."

"Thank you." Libby beamed with pleasure as she walked with Jill to the edge of the pond. She sat on the bench and slipped on her skates that Kevin had brought out earlier.

"Elizabeth!"

She looked up, the laces dangling from her fingers, to find Kevin on the edge of the pond. He looked almost round in his blue snowmobile suit. He pushed his glasses against his round face.

"You look just like a valentine!" he said with a laugh. "Will you be my valentine?"

She laughed and said she would be. Just last year if he'd said that she'd have knocked him flat. Now she knew he was teasing her because he loved her. She laughed again as he skated off to join Paul Noteboom.

"I'm ready," said Jill, carefully standing up. She held her hand out to Libby, then together they went on the ice.

Libby skated awkwardly for a minute, then steadied herself, one hand on Jill's arm, the other out for balance. She saw the flames of the bonfire and heard the laughter around her. This was her day!

A picture of herself locked in her small, untidy bedroom flashed in her mind. On her eleventh birthday she'd been sent to her room for swearing, then locked in because she'd said she wouldn't stay in. The family she'd been living with hadn't remembered her birthday at all. Could she be the same girl? She shook her head slightly. No, she was not. Chuck had said that when she'd accepted Jesus as her Savior and Lord that she'd been given a new spirit. He had showed her the Scripture that said she was a new creature in Christ and that the old things were passed away and all things were new. She was not that old Libby Dobbs! In Christ she was the new Elizabeth Gail!

She jumped as someone caught her hand. She looked, then smiled at Adam Feuder.

"Skate with me, Elizabeth," he said with a smile.

She nodded, then glanced at Jill. Libby's heart sank at the sad expression on Jill's face. Libby knew that Jill wanted to skate with Adam more than anything.

Libby told Jill she'd talk to her later and skated away with Adam. He was several inches taller than she was and he looked handsome in his dark brown coat with the sheepskin lining.

"I like your stuff," he said, motioning to her new outfit. Libby smiled and told him how happy she was to have it and how surprised she'd been when Vera and Susan had given it to her.

"Wait until you see what else you're getting," said Adam with a low laugh.

Libby stumbled and would've fallen if Adam hadn't gripped her tighter. "What am I getting?" How could there be more?

"I'm not telling, but I know you'll like your gifts."

Libby wanted to twirl around the pond and leap and glide, but knew if she let go of Adam she'd fall flat on her back.

By the time Chuck rang the bell, saying that it was time to go to the house, Libby's legs were weak and trembly. Someday she'd be able to skate like Brenda Wilkens and do all the fancy skating that impressed everyone.

Libby glanced at Jill several times as she took off her skates. Jill was very quiet and refused to look in Libby's direction. Libby bit the inside of her bottom lip. Adam had skated with her and Jill was probably jealous. Before Libby could say anything, Jill walked away from her and joined April and May as they hurried toward the house. With a sigh Libby followed.

"Libby!"

She looked to her left where the voice had come from, but whoever it was stood in the darkness just outside the light area. "Who is it?"

"I need your help!"

Libby's heart almost leaped through her jacket. Was this the voice of the caller? "What do you want? Come in the light so I can see you!"

"Elizabeth, walk with me."

She turned to find Chuck waiting for her across the yard, looking flushed with exertion. She glanced toward the shadows. "Come out where I can see you and I'll help you." She waited and there was no answer. Chuck called again so she ran to him. Should she say anything about the person in the dark? Maybe someone was only teasing her. If it was someone in need, he'd be gone if she and Chuck went back to help.

Had it been Mother?

"What is it, Elizabeth? You look very pale." Chuck looked down at her as they stopped just outside the back door. Voices from inside the back porch drifted out.

"Dad, did you talk to Mother and tell her to stay away tonight?"

He nodded. "She said she wouldn't even consider coming here."

Libby sighed in relief. She'd have to forget about the person in the dark and she'd forget about Mother. It was time to open the gifts and blow out the birthday candles and cut the cake.

Later in the basement Libby stood beside the table decorated with white paper and red hearts. A large bouquet of pink, red, and white carnations sat next to a large package that was also wrapped in pink, red, and white. Libby's heart raced and her fingers itched to tear off the red bow. What was inside the box?

Vera lit the thirteen red candles on the cake, then stepped back. "Elizabeth, make a wish and blow them out."

Libby stepped close as everyone sang "Happy Birthday." She closed her eyes and wished that the Johnsons would adopt her soon.

"Blow them out before they start the cake on fire," said Kevin with a hearty laugh.

Libby leaned forward and blew. The candles flickered and all went out but one.

"Libby has a boyfriend! Libby has a boyfriend!" chanted Toby, swinging his arms.

She blushed and wouldn't look around. What if she accidently looked at a boy and he thought she thought he was her boyfriend?

"Open the box, Elizabeth," said Chuck, motioning toward the gift.

Libby's fingers trembled as she tugged on the ribbon, then pulled down the paper. Her heart leaped and she stared around at everyone with tears blurring her vision. "Is this really for me?"

Susan laughed and squeezed Libby's arm. "We all went in together and got it for you. It was Jill's idea."

Libby found Jill and smiled, but Jill only nodded stiffly. "Thank you all very much!" Carefully Libby reached in the box and lifted out an cassette tape player. She set it beside the box, then looked and found several small gifts. She opened them quickly, hardly believing this was all for her.

"Oh! Tapes!" She looked at them and found two of contemporary gospel groups and two of piano music.

"Look at this one," said Vera, touching a tape next to Libby's left hand.

Libby picked it up, then gasped, her eyes wide. "It's Rachael Avery in concert! Oh, my!" Libby pressed the tape to her as she thought about the beautiful music her piano teacher made on the piano.

Finally Libby looked around the room, her cheeks reddened. "I have never had such a wonderful birthday party. Thank you all for coming and thank you for this gift." She thought of all the things she could say but the words wouldn't come. She was glad when Vera said it was time to eat.

Libby stood beside her table and watched her guests line up for food at the counter. She would never, never forget this birthday!

FIVE
Great news

Libby bit into the pizza, then pulled the piece away.
Mozzarella cheese made long strings before it snapped
apart. Libby picked a piece of pepperoni off the top and
pushed it into her mouth. She saw a smear of sauce on
Toby's chin. Ben picked up his piece of pizza, then just
held it as he told about lifesaving procedure in
swimming class. When he stopped talking Susan said
that Joe was coming over, but Vera said he wasn't.
Libby thought for sure Susan was going to burst into
tears right at the supper table.

"I'll sure be glad when I'm thirteen!" Susan flopped
back in her chair with a pout. "Libby's been thirteen
only two weeks and she can do anything she wants!"

Libby stared at Susan in surprise. What on earth did
she mean?

"I bet Libby could have a boyfriend if she wanted!"
Susan's face was red and she looked accusingly at Libby.

"This is not the time to discuss this," said Chuck
firmly. "We want a pleasant meal without bickering."
He reached over and rubbed Susan's cheek. "You'll be

old enough to go with boys soon, honey. We're not stopping you from seeing Joe. We're saying you can be with him one evening a week. When you're dating, you'll be going out only one night a week." He smiled at her and she finally smiled back.

Libby sighed in relief. She didn't want Susan upset the rest of the evening. Libby drank the last of her glass of cold water, then dabbed her mouth with the napkin. She looked up to find Chuck and Vera looking at her as if they knew something exciting. Her heart raced and she sat very still.

"We have wonderful news, family," said Chuck, leaning forward. His hazel eyes were bright with excitement. "Today we received the phone call that we've been waiting for."

Libby licked her dry lips as she stared at Chuck.

"The judge finally set the day for the adoption." He laughed as he looked at Libby. "On March first you and Vera and I go to court for the judge to give the final word on your adoption. On the first day of March you will legally be Elizabeth Gail Johnson!"

Libby pressed her hand to her mouth as everyone shouted happily. The first day of March was Thursday! Was she dreaming? Oh! Thursday!

"Sunday we'll have an open house to celebrate," said Vera. "I called Grandma and Grandpa already and they said they could come."

Libby's head spun and she felt as if she'd burst with happiness. She was going to be Elizabeth Gail Johnson! After Thursday she'd no longer be Dobb the Slob, the name that Brenda Wilkens had given her when they were enemies.

"Rachel Avery said that she'd come to entertain the

37

guests." Vera sat with her elbows on the table, her hands clasped, and her eyes sparkling.

"She is?" Libby couldn't take it all in. Could this be happening to her? *Was* she dreaming? She'd better not be!

"Will Uncle Luke and Scottie come?" asked Kevin.

Vera nodded and Libby thought that Sunday seemed too far off. She tingled all over and could barely sit still while the others talked excitedly about the party.

Suddenly Libby pushed back her chair and jumped up. "I want to tell Jill my good news. Is it all right if I call her now?"

"Go right ahead," said Vera. "If she wants to help us plan the party and help us decorate, she is welcome to."

In the family room Libby picked up the phone to dial Jill's number. Libby's hand shook so much she could barely dial. Just before she dialed the last number, she stopped. Jill had been very unfriendly since the birthday party. Maybe she wouldn't want to talk or help plan a party.

Slowly Libby replaced the receiver. It would be better to see Jill on the bus tomorrow and talk to her face to face.

The fire crackled loudly as Libby walked to the window and looked out into the darkness. Suddenly she stopped smiling and frowned. How could she be so happy to break so completely from Mother? Libby turned from the window and walked to the couch and sank down on the edge, her hands between her knees, her shoulders drooping. She was learning to love with God's love. Yet, she could happily be adopted by this family and never think of Mother again. Was it right to feel this way?

Libby looked up as Chuck walked in. She glanced quickly away from him.

"What's wrong with my girl?" he asked softly as he sat beside her and took her hands in his.

She cleared her throat and shrugged.

"Tell me, Elizabeth." He sat back and pulled her with him.

She twisted around and looked into his face. She thought her heart would burst with love for him. "Mother has no kids. What will she do without any kids?"

Chuck took Libby's face in his hands. "Compassion for your mother is from the Lord, honey. Never feel guilty or bad because you feel this way. We'll pray for your mother, but at this point she is not capable of handling anyone but herself. She is better off with you here because that leaves her free of responsibility for you. She can't handle it right now, nor could she in the past. Don't feel guilty because you've at last found happiness. Hang onto your happiness and pray that your mother finds it someday, too."

Libby felt tears slip down her cheeks as Chuck pulled her close and held her. She leaned against him as he prayed for Mother.

The next morning Libby watched as Jill stepped onto the school bus. Libby gasped and just stared as Jill walked down the aisle and sat beside her. Jill was wearing makeup! And her hair was cut and curled! What had happened to Jill Noteboom?

"Close your mouth, Libby," said Jill under her breath as the bus lurched and pulled away from the Noteboom driveway.

Libby snapped her mouth closed.

"Well, aren't you going to say anything?" Jill tugged

her skirt in place, then turned to Libby. "Say something!"

"I . . . I can't."

"I've lost ten pounds in the last two weeks. By the end of the school year I'll weigh just what I should. And then Adam won't look at me as if I don't exist."

"I like you the way you were, Jill. Why do you have to change?"

She fluffed her brown hair. "There is more to life than hiding away every day to write. There is more to life than being a giant. I won't mind being tall once I am slender and gorgeous. Adam will grow and he won't mind that I'm this tall."

Libby groaned and slipped low in her seat. How could Jill do this? Jill was not Susan! Susan was always more interested in boys than in anything else, but not Jill. Why did things have to change?

Jill jabbed Libby's arm. "You don't have to be jealous of me. And I won't be jealous of you. Just stay away from Adam."

"Adam!" shrieked Libby.

"Did you want me, Elizabeth?" asked Adam in surprise.

She turned and looked at Adam two seats behind them. She shook her head and turned around again, her face burning hot.

"Now he knows we're talking about him," said Jill impatiently as she frowned at Libby. "Keep your voice down, will you?"

"Sorry." Libby hunched her shoulders and made a face. Suddenly she remembered her good news. She opened her mouth to tell Jill, but Jill turned to her just then.

"I could lose all this weight by the end of the next

month if I quit eating altogether. Just think how wonderful I'll look." She lifted her chin and posed like a model. "What do you think, Libby?"

"I like you the way you are." She smiled and clasped her hands. "I have fantastic news, Jill."

"I'm going to buy all new clothes. Daddy said he'd give me the money. He said his royalty check should come in April. I think I should buy a makeup case, too."

"Will you listen to me, Jill?"

The bus stopped at the railroad tracks and everyone was silent. Jill folded her hands in her lap and sat quietly. Libby wanted to shake her. The bus doors closed and the driver shifted into first gear and drove across the tracks.

"Mom said she'd teach me how to use makeup to make the most of myself. She even thinks I'm pretty."

Libby groaned and sank down in her seat. Maybe she could tell Jill the good news sometime next year, or whenever Jill decided to come back to earth.

SIX
Elizabeth Gail Johnson

Libby leaned against the back seat of the car with the folded paper pressed against her heart.

Vera looked over her shoulder and smiled. "You are now Elizabeth Gail Johnson! Ms. Kremeen's statement didn't have any bad effect on the judge. He knew you belonged to us!"

Libby opened the paper and looked at it. She was officially, legally, and happily Elizabeth Gail Johnson! All the way home she held the paper.

Chuck pulled into the driveway and Rex raced toward the car, barking a welcome. Libby waved. Did he know that she was really a part of the family now? She wanted to shout out the news so everyone for miles around could hear. Would Jill listen this time to the good news? Of could she would! Weren't they best friends?

"Here comes the school bus," said Chuck as he stood beside the car.

Cold air blew against Libby as she scrambled out. She stood beside Vera and impatiently waited for the kids to race up the driveway. Just for a minute she wanted to run and hide. What if they weren't excited about her news? What if they said they wished she'd stayed Libby Dobbs? She pushed the thoughts aside. She was glad when Vera caught her hand and held it firmly.

"I'm blessed to have such a precious family," she said with a catch in her voice. "Every family should have five wonderful children."

Libby puffed up with pride. *She* was a part of the family! Never again would she have to explain why her last name was different than the others in the family. Now, her last name was Johnson. No one would ever ask her how it felt to be an aid kid. She'd never be sent to another foster home to be kicked around and treated with anger and hatred. She lifted her eyes to the bright blue sky and silently said thank you to her heavenly Father. Last year the Johnsons had prayed her into the family, saying that she would be adopted. Libby nodded. It had come to pass!

"Elizabeth!" shouted Ben and Kevin as they raced toward her, their hair flopping, their faces red.

"Libby! Libby!" cried Susan and Toby as they raced toward her.

"Elizabeth is officially part of the family," said Chuck happily as Susan grabbed Libby and hugged her close. She smelled like Vera's perfume.

"You are really and truly my sister now, Libby," Susan said with tears in her blue eyes. "I'm glad. I love you, Libby."

"I love you." Libby hugged her again, then turned to find Ben waiting to hug her close. She was almost as tall as he. His hair tickled her nose and she almost sneezed.

Toby and Kevin hugged her and Chuck said it was

time to go inside and get out of the cold. Libby felt so warm and loved, she didn't think she'd ever be cold again.

A horse nickered from the pen by the barn and Libby turned to find Snowball standing with her head over the fence. "I'll be in in a minute, Dad," Libby said over her shoulder, then she ran across the yard to Snowball. "Oh, Snowball! I'm so happy!"

Libby hugged her white filly, then kissed her on the face between the eyes. Snowball looked fat and fluffy with her thick coat of winter hair. She bobbed her head up and down and seemed to say that she loved Libby, too.

"I belong to the family, Snowball. My name is Elizabeth Gail Johnson! I really belong here now!" Snowball nickered and Libby laughed. She stood with her arm over Snowball's neck and talked to her for a long time. "I guess I'd better get to the house now. I'll see you later when I feed you, Snowball. I'm sorry I didn't have a treat for you in my pocket."

Libby said good-bye again, then turned to walk across the yard. She stopped half-way, noticing for the first time a strange car parked beside Chuck's. A woman stood beside the car and Libby's legs seemed to turn to water. She wanted to scream, but her voice was locked in her tight throat. The woman was Mother!

She walked toward Libby with an angry scowl on her face.

Suddenly Libby gasped, her eyes wide. It wasn't Mother after all! It was Phyllis LaDere. She had the same bleached blonde hair and wore the same type of tight clothes. What was Phyllis LaDere doing here?

She stopped in front of Libby, her eyes narrowed. "Where's Tammy? You tell that girl of mine to get herself out here so she can go home with me."

"Tammy?"

"Don't act so dumb, Libby! You remember your cousin Tammy, don't you? I didn't think you could ever forget your cousin who looks just like you. Now, tell that disobedient girl of mine to get out here!"

Libby finally found her voice. She doubled her fists and lifted her pointed chin. "Tammy isn't here and has never been here! I haven't seen her or talked to her since last spring when she was at Grandma LaDere's home."

Phyllis stepped closer and Libby smelled her strong perfume and stale tobacco. "You're lying! Tammy called you twice that I know of. I saw your name and number on a piece of paper, and I saw her dial the number and talk!" Phyllis narrowed her eyes. "She hung up fast enough when she knew I was watching her."

Libby stumbled back, her heart racing. So, Tammy has been the mysterious caller! Had she also been the person who had asked for help the night of the birthday party? But why hadn't she just stepped out in the open and talked? Why hadn't she said on the phone who she was? There was something strange going on.

"If you don't get Tammy out here right now I'm going to march right up to the front door of your house and ring the doorbell. I'll tell that fancy family of yours just what I think of them!" Phyllis turned toward the house, but Libby caught her arm.

"Leave them alone. None of us knows where Tammy is. She is not here and I don't think she'll ever be here."

Phyllis jerked free. "I'll see for myself. I sure can't trust your word about anything. No daughter of Marie LaDere Dobbs can be trusted."

Libby squared her shoulders. "My parents are Chuck and Vera Johnson and I have a paper to prove it!"

Phyllis laughed a hard, brittle laugh. "You have LaDere blood in your veins, Libby, and don't you ever think you'll be different from the rest of us. We're all alike. In a few more years you'll be walking the streets with no home and no one to care. You'll be living with any man who'll have you."

Libby clamped her hand over her ears. "No! No, no, no!" Was Phyllis LaDere right? Libby shook her head. She couldn't be right! Libby backed away. She was going to be a famous concert pianist and everyone would know her and want to hear her perform.

"What's going on out here?"

Libby ran to Chuck and flung her arms around his waist and pressed her face against his rough farm coat.

"Marie Dobbs?" he asked hesitantly. "No, you're not Marie Dobbs. Who are you and why are you here?"

"You must be Chuck Johnson. You don't look much like your brother Luke, but I do look like my sister Marie. I'm Phyllis LaDere and I've come to get my daughter Tammy. She ran away this morning. I know that she's been trying to get out here to stay with Libby. I want her back right now."

Chuck lifted Libby's face. "Do you know about this?"

"No," she whispered, shivering.

"Tammy isn't here. If she comes, we'll see that she gets home. Elizabeth and I must go in now. I hope you find your daughter."

Libby watched Phyllis hesitate, then walk to her car and drive away. Libby shivered again and Chuck said she was safe and had nothing to fear. He walked with her into the house and the warm air enveloped her completely.

She forced thoughts of Phyllis LaDere away each

time they tried to enter her mind for the next three days. On Sunday Libby didn't have time to think about anything except going to church and then coming home for the open house. Vera had said about two hundred people were expected and Libby was amazed that even two people would be interested enough to want to celebrate her adoption.

Just as the grandfather clock bonged two, Rachael Avery walked in and said she was glad for Libby.

"I'll play my best for you and your guests," Rachael said as she sat at the piano in the family room. "I'll tell anyone who asks about your musical ability that someday you'll be a famous concert pianist."

Libby laughed in delight. "Thank you." She stood beside the piano and watched Rachael's long fingers fly over the keys. Rachael's long black hair hung around her slender shoulders and down her back. Her blue dress almost touched the floor. Diamond earrings hung from her ears and swayed gently each time she moved her head.

Just then Jill grabbed Libby's arm and pulled her into the hall away from a crowd of people who were filing into the family room to listen to Rachael.

"Why didn't you tell me the most important thing in your life, Libby? I thought best friends weren't supposed to keep secrets from each other."

Libby couldn't be angry. She laughed and explained that she'd tried to tell Jill more than once. "You've been thinking about Adam Feuder most of the time, Jill."

She shrugged. "I know. I can't help myself." She rubbed her hand down her skirt. "I love him, Libby. One of these days he'll love me."

Libby rolled her eyes. She was sure glad she wasn't in

love with anyone. It would be terrible to hurt the way Jill was hurting. Before she could say more, someone called to her and she turned to find Brian and Lisa Parr with baby Amy.

"Congratulations, Libby," said Lisa, hugging Libby.

"We brought you a gift," said Brian as he tugged a handful of his hair out of Amy's hand. "It's on the table in the living room. Susan put it there for us."

"Thank you," said Libby, remembering Kevin's teasing this morning. He'd said that this would be like a baby shower, because Libby was the new "baby" in the family.

Amy leaned toward Libby with her hands out.

Libby took her and talked to her until she wanted to get down. Music from the family room filled the air along with voices.

Several minutes later Libby walked with Jill to the living room. Libby gasped at the stack of gifts on the table that Vera and Susan had set up and decorated.

"*I* should get adopted," said Jill softly as she walked around the table. "I didn't get to enjoy all the stuff I got at my baby shower."

Libby touched a package with a white ribbon as she thought about all the years that she'd never received a gift for Christmas or her birthday. This seemed too good to be true. She thought of all the boys and girls who never received even one gift and she wanted to find them and share with them. Someday she would. She'd look for kids who had nothing and had no one to love them and she'd love them and give them gifts.

"Let's see if Adam came yet," said Jill, walking toward the door.

Libby followed her, then stopped as Lisa Parr hurried toward her.

"Have you seen Amy?" asked Lisa urgently. "We've looked all over for her! Did you see her?"

"No, but we'll look for her," said Libby. How could they find a little girl among all these people? What if she'd walked outdoors when someone was walking in? Libby hurried toward the stairs as she tried to stop the nervous shivers that ran up and down her spine.

Where was baby Amy?

SEVEN
The search

Libby stopped in the upstairs hallway and tilted her head, tapping her chin thoughtfully. Amy was not hiding in any bedroom or bathroom up here. Where was the best place to look next? Had Jill had any success downstairs? Maybe Lisa or Brian had already found Amy.

Strains of a Beethoven sonata drifted upstairs and Libby wanted to be in the family room right now to listen and watch Rachael Avery play.

Just as Libby reached the bottom of the stairs, Aunt Gwen stepped from the family room.

"Libby!" She rushed to Libby and hugged her warmly.

Libby laughed softly, thinking how strange it was to have this woman who had once been Miss Miller, hugging her this way. Miss Miller had been her caseworker since she was five, then she'd married Uncle Luke. "When did you get here?"

"A few minutes ago. I waved to you outdoors, but you didn't see me."

Libby frowned. "Outdoors? I've been upstairs looking for baby Amy Parr."

"But I saw you, and so did Luke and Scottie." Gwen studied Libby thoughtfully. "Is something troubling you that you want to talk about?"

Libby backed away, her chin up. "I am not lying, Miss Miller!"

Gwen smiled and touched Libby's arm lightly. "I'm sorry, honey. I don't mean to imply that you're lying and I don't mean to sound like your caseworker." Suddenly she laughed a soft, tinkling laugh. "Oh, Libby! Isn't this marvelous?" She waved her hand in an arc. "God has been very good to you. God is good! He has given you many marvelous things and this family is one of them." Gwen's brown hair curled prettily around her face. Libby liked her camel beige dress and high-heeled shoes.

"I'm glad I'm adopted." A rush of happiness enveloped Libby and she wanted to dance around the hall, shouting her new name at the top of her lungs. Just then she caught sight of Jill. "Oh! I must find Amy Parr. I'll talk to you later, Aunt Gwen." Libby liked calling Miss Miller Aunt Gwen and was glad that she had married Uncle Luke.

Libby hurried to catch Jill, but Jill looked at her, glared, and practically ran to the basement steps. What was wrong with Jill? Libby stopped at the steps with a frown, but before she could go down Lisa called to her. Libby turned and Lisa seemed very upset.

"I thought you were going to look for Amy, Libby."

"I did."

"Outdoors?"

What was this? First Aunt Gwen and now Lisa. "I was upstairs looking for her and she wasn't there."

Lisa wrung her hands. "Where is she? I don't want to

tell everyone and ruin the day." Lisa's eyes widened. "Maybe Susan has her! I'll find Susan and ask her!" Lisa whirled around, her long hair flying out, and ran toward the back porch.

Libby hesitated, then walked to the basement. Maybe Susan was in the basement instead of outdoors. Or maybe Jill could answer a few questions.

Libby's flowered dress brushed against the bannister as she walked down. She heard the Ping-Pong ball being hit back and forth. Someone laughed and others talked softly.

On the last step Libby stopped and looked around. The room seemed as full as it had on her birthday. She saw Jill's head above several girls' heads near the fireplace. Had Jill really frowned at her? Or had Jill been deep in thought and not seen her?

Several people congratulated her as she pushed her way through to Jill's side.

"I see you finally came in," said Jill sharply.

"Did you find Amy?"

Jill shook her head. "At least I tried and that's more than I can say for you."

Libby doubled her fists at her sides. "What do you mean by that?" She would not yell at Jill or punch her in the nose!

"I saw you, Libby." Jill grabbed Libby's arm and dragged her to a deserted area of the basement. Libby felt as if a million eyes were on her and she flushed uncomfortably. "I saw you outdoors, Libby—with Adam! I thought you agreed to leave him alone!" Jill pushed her face close to Libby's, and Libby felt her warm breath on her cheek. "I saw you flirting with

Adam! How do you think that makes me feel? How can my very best friend flirt with the man I'm in love with?"

"You're not making sense, Jill. I was upstairs looking for Amy, and I didn't find her."

"But I saw you outdoors!"

Libby narrowed her eyes. "Something strange is going on. I'm going to find out what it is right now!" She turned and forced her way to the stairs and ran up. Suddenly she stopped. Brian Parr stood in the kitchen door with Amy sleeping in his arms.

He walked to Libby with a smile across his face. "Amy was behind the couch in the living room with her blanket, fast asleep. Thanks for looking for her."

"I'm glad she's all right."

"Lisa went to look for you a minute ago to let you know we found Amy. Did she find you?"

"No. Right now I have to go outside. Tell Lisa I know you have Amy." Libby forced a smile and hurried to the back porch for her jacket. She slipped on her boots and pulled on her new red and white jacket. She would see who was outdoors and end this mystery right now!

Cold air blew against her as she walked away from the shelter of the house. Several kids were having a snowball fight. Goosy Poosy honked from where he was locked up in the chicken pen. Libby knew the big white goose wanted to be in the yard where he could act like he was king. He thought he owned the Johnson farm. She saw him flap his wings and honk again and she laughed. Maybe he *was* king of the farm.

Libby walked toward the doghouse. Rex jumped up and strained against his chain, barking happily. "Sorry, Rex, but I can't turn you loose." She hugged him. He smelled warm and dusty.

She talked to him awhile, then walked away toward the back of the chicken house. Just then a girl standing alone nearby turned and Libby stopped dead. Was she looking in a mirror?

"Tammy?" whispered Libby, swallowing hard.

"Hi, Libby." Tammy walked slowly toward her. Her coat was red and she had on dark blue pants. Her hair was curled like Libby's.

"What are you doing here?" Libby's voice came out in a harsh whisper and she couldn't move.

Tammy pushed her hair away from her face. "I came to see you, cousin. I learned where you lived from Grandma LaDere, and I decided to come see you."

"Your mother was here looking for you a few days ago." Libby felt as if she was in a bad dream and she tried to force herself awake. What if this wasn't a dream? What if Tammy was here to tell everyone about the terrible family she'd been born into?

"I ran away." Tammy thrust her hands in her pockets and hunched her slender shoulders. "I can't go back, Libby! But I don't know what to do! Is there a Johnson family who would adopt me?" Giant tears filled her eyes and slowly slipped down her pale cheeks. Abruptly she turned away. "I need your help. I don't have anyone else to ask."

Libby didn't know if she should turn and run or take Tammy in her arms and pat her on the back the way Vera did to her. "What can I do, Tammy?"

Just then Chuck called to Libby, telling her it was time to open the gifts.

Libby waved to let him know she'd heard, then turned back to Tammy, but Tammy was disappearing behind a large tree and Libby couldn't follow or call to her.

Libby kicked a clump of snow, then slowly walked to the house. She reached the back door the same time Adam did.

"Did you see that girl who looks like you, Elizabeth?" Adam held open the door and she walked in.

"She came for help, Adam. Please, don't tell anyone that she was here until I can talk to Dad."

He nodded. "I'll help her if I can."

Libby turned from hanging up her jacket to find Jill standing there. Before Libby could speak, Jill turned and walked stiffly away. Libby's heart sank. How would she ever convince Jill that she wasn't trying to win Adam's love? She squared her shoulders. She couldn't think about that now. She was going to open all the gifts on the table in the living room. Shivers of excitement ran up and down her back and she giggled nervously. All those gifts were from people who were glad that she was now Elizabeth Gail Johnson.

At the gift table Libby forced back thoughts of Tammy and Jill and smiled at Chuck on one side of her and Vera on the other. The room was packed with people and Libby managed to smile at them. Her hands shook as she took the gift Chuck handed to her.

"Elizabeth and Vera and I want to thank everyone for making this a very special day. Thank you for the gifts and the love. This is a very happy time for us and we're glad we could share it with you." Chuck grinned and nodded for Libby to start opening the gift in her hand.

Several minutes later she stood beside the table as the guests filed past to speak to her and to admire her gifts. She could barely breathe in her excitement. The table was filled with clothes, jewelry, books, records, cassette tapes, a camera from Uncle Luke and Aunt

Gwen, perfume, and even sweet-smelling bath soap and bath towels.

Vera spoke her name and she turned into Vera's arms. "Welcome to our family, Elizabeth Johnson. I love you. I will always be the best mother I know how to be to you."

Libby sniffed back tears and kissed Vera's soft cheek. Today had to be the best day of her life.

EIGHT
Toby's day

Libby poured the cocoa into the creamed sugar, eggs, and butter. The mixer turned fast and forced the brown cocoa around and around until the entire cake batter was chocolate brown. She looked over her shoulder at Vera and smiled. "I'm sure glad there's no school today. It gives Toby the whole day to celebrate his tenth birthday." She remembered how he'd looked the first day he'd come to the Johnsons'. He'd stood just inside the door with his thumb in his mouth and a scared look on his face. He'd hated Libby at first because she looked a little like his mean sister, but now he loved her. She felt warm all over thinking about Toby's love and the love of the entire Johnson family.

Vera poured herself a cup of coffee and sat at the table, the cup between her hands. "Chuck said he'd come home from the store early so he can join the boys. He's going to take all of them in the sleigh. Ben said he'd hitch Jack and Dan up about three and be ready."

Libby knew how much fun it was to ride in the sleigh with the big gray horses pulling it, but she didn't mind not going today on Toby's day. Several boys were coming at two to go skating and sledding. Kevin said maybe they could choose teams and have a snowball fight.

Carefully Libby poured the cake batter into two round tins. She set the bowl down, then rubbed her finger around it and licked it off. It tasted delicious. She rubbed her finger on a napkin and set the pans in the hot oven. "Where's Susan? She usually helps with the baking."

Vera shook her head with a frown. "She's doing her math. She's been dropping behind in it lately. Joe Wilkens is on her mind entirely too much."

"Just tell her to stop thinking about him." Libby stood with her hands on her hips.

Vera laughed softly. "That's easy enough to say, Elizabeth, but not easy to do. Susan wants to think about Joe. She loves him."

Libby rolled her eyes. Susan and Jill both were sure dumb to want to be in love with a boy.

"It's different with you, Elizabeth. Your mind is on the piano. You know where you're going, but Susan doesn't. Right now all she wants to do is be a wife and mother. There's nothing wrong with that, but I do want Susan to know positively that that's what she wants to do with her life before she does it." Vera sighed and rubbed her finger around the rim of her coffee cup. "I think it was easier to settle problems for Susan when she was younger. I'm glad we have the Lord to help us. He'll give me wisdom, so I really shouldn't worry or fret." Finally she looked up with a smile and Libby felt much better. "I refuse to worry over this, Libby! Susan will follow God's will for her life!"

Later as Libby pulled on her ski pants and jacket she

determined that she'd follow God's will for her life, too. She'd never let anything stop her from doing what God wanted her to do. She'd make God and the Johnsons proud of her.

The smell of the baking birthday cake filled the porch. Vera had said she'd watch it if Libby wanted to go outdoors to see Snowball and Rex.

Libby could hear the boys in the basement, cleaning it for Toby's party. If they weren't done when she came in she'd help them. Toby shouldn't have to work hard on his birthday. She smiled as she thought of his beaming, freckled face when he'd come down for breakfast that morning.

"I'm glad they closed school special for my birthday today," he'd said with a laugh.

Chuck had pulled Toby close in a bear hug. "They planned the teachers' in-service just right, didn't they?"

Libby laughed under her breath as she walked into the snowy backyard. Rex barked from his doghouse and Libby called happily to him. Goosy Poosy honked indignantly from the chicken pen where Kevin had left him that morning.

A whirlwind of snow blew along the plowed driveway. Snowball nickered from the pen beside the horse barn. Libby flung her arms wide and ran through the snow toward the barn. Cold air stung her nose and turned her cheeks red. She watched a bird fly to a branch of a tree, then fly away again.

Snowball bobbed her head up and down and Libby stopped beside the fence to talk to her. Finally she walked inside the barn to see Jack and Dan. She reached to turn on the light and someone grabbed her arm. She shrieked, then looked over her shoulder expecting to see Ben or Joe or Adam. The man gripping her arm was a stranger and her heart leaped in fear. He was about a head taller and looked very strong. A black mustache almost covered his top lip and his teeth looked yellow as he opened his mouth to speak.

"Your mother wants you home with her right now! If you make any noise I'll knock you out and carry you to my car."

Mother wanted her! Was this Mother's plan all along? Didn't she know this would be kidnapping now that she belonged to the Johnsons? "I'm not going with you!" She jerked but he twisted her arm around and brought it up tight behind her and the pain made her gasp. If she moved, her arm would snap. "Why does Mother want me?"

"Very funny." He forced her toward the back door of the barn. "We don't want no one to see us when we leave. My car is parked alongside the road near that big white house."

She knew he meant the Wilkenses'. Maybe Joe would see what was happening and help her.

Dan neighed and the man jumped, loosening his grip. "Can that horse get out?"

"Don't tell me you're afraid of horses!"

"Don't get smart with me, girl. Just answer me."

"He can't get out of his stall."

The man wiped his brow and swallowed hard. "Barns give me the creeps. Let's get out of here." He pushed open the back door and Snowball ran toward them, nickering at Libby. The man jumped aside and Libby dashed around the barn and leaped over the fence into the backyard. Her heart raced with fear and she expected a hand to grab her at any minute. She stumbled over a clump of snow and almost fell, then caught herself and dashed to the back door and jerked it open. She fell inside and closed and locked the door, then leaned against it, her chest rising and falling.

Why was Mother so desperate to get her back now? Her mouth felt too dry to talk and her legs too weak to support her. She sank to the floor, her back tight against the door.

Who was that man? Was he getting her as a favor to Mother? Why, oh why, did Mother want her now? Was she angry about the adoption?

"I must tell Chuck," she whispered painfully as she forced herself to her feet. The porch seemed to spin and she clutched the doorknob for support. Finally she took a step forward. She'd call Chuck and tell him, and he'd take care of everything. She stopped, her hand at her mouth. How could she do this and ruin Toby's day? But what if that man stayed outdoors and grabbed her at chore time tonight? What should she do? Maybe the man had left. She could run up to Ben's room and look out his window. If the car was still parked on the edge of the road, she'd call Chuck; if not, she wouldn't.

Susan called to her from the family room but she kept going.

"I need help with my math," shouted Susan impatiently.

Libby looked down the steps at her, then turned and ran into Ben's room. She pulled aside the heavy blue drape and looked out. A heavy truck drove past, leaving the road empty. No car sat at the side of the road near the Wilkenses' place.

With a relieved sigh Libby turned away, then stopped when she found Susan standing in the doorway with a puzzled look on her pretty face.

"What are you up to this time, Libby?"

She looked down at her stocking feet, then at Susan. "Why should I be up to anything?"

Susan laughed dryly, and threw her hands wide. "I know you. Remember?"

"It just so happens I needed to look out the window. I wanted to check on something I saw on the road. It wasn't anything. Are you satisfied?" Libby pushed past Susan, then turned. "If you want help with math, then let's get to work. You have to get done or you won't be able to enjoy Toby's birthday and this school vacation."

Susan's mouth dropped open, then she giggled. "Thanks, Libby. I wish I could do it as easily as you."

Libby shrugged with a grin. "Me, too. Since you can't, let's get to it." She turned, then winced. Her shoulder hurt because the strange man had twisted her arm so hard. She would not think about that. Tomorrow she'd tell Chuck what happened. He'd take care of everything. Mother would never again bother her or send someone to take her away.

Just as Libby helped Susan with the last math problem the phone rang. Libby answered, then wished she hadn't as she remembered the strange calls she'd received before.

"I want to talk to Libby."

"This is Libby." Was this woman someone she knew?

"This is Phyllis LaDere."

Libby almost dropped the phone. She swallowed hard. "Yes?"

"I know Tammy was there yesterday. I want her home immediately. You tell her for me. I'll get the police on this if she doesn't get here shortly. You tell her that."

"What . . ." The phone clicked, then buzzed sharply and Libby slowly hung up. She sank to a chair.

"What's wrong, Libby?" asked Susan. "You look scared. Who was on the phone?"

Libby opened her mouth, then closed it. Once again she'd have to keep quiet so she wouldn't ruin Toby's day. She stood up, saying it wasn't that important, then walked out.

By the time Toby's guests came, Libby felt more relaxed. She would not go out alone to do chores later. Then, even if the man came back, he'd be afraid to show himself.

When Toby opened his gifts and blew out his candles, Libby joined in with the laughter and the singing of "Happy Birthday."

Toby stood at the gift table while Chuck snapped a picture of him. He looked very happy. He didn't stop smiling even when Kevin and Paul Noteboom stopped at the table to look at everything.

Libby jumped when Vera spoke at her side.

"What's wrong, honey? You've been nervous most of the day. I think the last few days have been hard on you."

For a minute Libby thought about telling about the man and the phone call, but she closed her mouth. Nothing was going to happen to her. She had no reason to be worried or nervous.

NINE
Tammy

Libby walked slowly around the water fountain at the shopping mall. She glanced at her watch to see that she still had a half hour before she had to meet Vera at Penney's.

Several boys ran past, shouting playfully. Libby wondered how it would feel to run up and down in the mall. She walked around a bench surrounded with plants, then stopped dead at the sight of Tammy LaDere.

"I saw you coming," said Tammy, quickly looking over her shoulder. "I need to talk to you. Please!"

"Are you in trouble?" Libby saw a woman look at them, then look again. She probably thought they were twins.

Tammy hesitated, then shrugged. "Nothing I can't handle, I guess." She sank down on the secluded bench and Libby sat beside here. "You made it, didn't you, Libby?" Tammy looked as if she was going to cry and Libby squirmed uncomfortably.

"Your mother's been looking for you, Tammy."

She leaned back with her arms folded tightly against

herself. "I know. And I don't care! I'll never go back! She doesn't care anything about me." She turned to Libby, her hands clasped tightly. "Can't the Johnsons adopt me, too? I want to live in the country with a nice family. I want to take piano lessons and go to the same school year after year!"

Libby gnawed the inside of her bottom lip as she tried to think of some way to help Tammy.

"Oh, Libby! I hate being a LaDere! I don't want to be like my mother or yours. I want to be like . . . like Vera Johnson."

Libby nodded. "Me, too," she said in a low, urgent voice. It would be terrible to be like Mother or Phyllis LaDere!

Tammy licked her lips, then brushed a piece of brown hair off her pale cheek. "Can you ask the Johnsons if I can live with them?"

Libby's mind whirled. Could she? Dare she? "I don't know."

Tammy sat up straight, her chin high. "You mean you won't! You hate me for what I did to you before. You hate me, don't you, Libby?"

Libby shook her head. "I don't hate you, Tammy. And I forgave you for stealing that gold chain and blaming me for it."

Tammy flushed and looked down at her legs. She wore blue jeans and old nylon sneakers. "You don't hate me, Libby?"

"Of course not!" Libby's eyes widened as she realized that right now she loved Tammy and wanted to do something to help her. "Tammy, why can't you go live with a friend for a while?"

"A friend? I don't have any friends here. We've only

lived here about six weeks. Sure, I know quite a few boys, but I won't live with any of them. I will not be like Mother!"

Libby took a deep breath. "I'll ask the Johnsons if you can stay there until you find a home. Dad will help you find something."

"Thank you! Thank you very much!" Tears slipped down Tammy's cheeks and she quickly brushed them away, laughing self-consciously. "I'll sneak home and get a few things, then get a ride there." She swallowed hard. "Mother and that man living with her will be gone sometime today. While they're gone, I'll get my stuff."

"Come right now with Vera and me and you can wear my clothes."

"Thanks, Libby, but I have special things that I want." Tammy stood up and smiled hesitantly. "You don't think the Johnsons will say no, do you?"

Libby pushed herself up. She was a little taller than Tammy but Tammy was not as thin. "They'll help you if I ask them to."

"You're so lucky! Why didn't someone take me and adopt me? I hate my life!" She doubled her fists at her sides and closed her eyes tightly.

Libby touched her arm and she jerked. "Tammy, come home with me right now and get your special things later. Please?"

Tammy looked at Libby a long time, then said, "OK, but first you talk to Vera Johnson, then come get me. I'll wait here. If you aren't back soon, then I'll know Vera said no."

Libby looked at her watch. "I have to meet Vera in ten minutes. You give us at least a half hour, but we'll be back. You don't have to worry about that at all. Vera will say yes."

"Are you sure?"

"Yes."

Tammy sighed and seemed to relax a little. "I'll wait for you. You won't forget where I am, will you?"

Libby laughed and shook her head. "The music store is over there and the water fountain and this. How can I forget?"

"I guess you can't." Tammy rubbed her hands on her jacket sleeves. "I'll wait one hour, but no longer!"

"We'll be here, Tammy. I promise." Libby smiled, then turned and walked away. Would Vera let Tammy go home with them? Of course she would! She'd let April and May Brakie stay. Vera liked helping others. She always said that love was an action word. Love helped others.

Libby hurried past three old women discussing something loudly and heatedly. Two little girls almost ran into Libby, but she jumped aside just in time. Busy shoppers hurried along, some happily, some sadly, and others tiredly.

Just outside Penney's Libby stopped to look at a little boy who was crying hard. "Are you lost?" she asked.

He looked up and sniffed. "I want my dad."

"Where is he?"

The boy shrugged as more tears rushed down his cheeks. "I want my dad!"

Libby looked around, then spotted a policeman walking slowly toward them. She hurried to him. "That little boy is lost. Can you help him?"

The man frowned as he pushed his cap back. "Take

him to the information booth and they'll call his dad over the speaker."

"Where's the booth?"

"About the middle of the mall at the Charles Street exit."

"But I have to meet my mom." My, but that sounded good! Her mom! "I have to meet her right now."

The policeman sighed and caught the little boy's hand. "Come with me and we'll find your dad."

"I don't want to go with you!" The boy tugged away, crying loudly. "I want my dad!"

Libby stood hesitantly, then hurried to the boy. "I'll take him to the information booth."

He stopped sobbing and threw himself against her, clinging to her leg. The policeman muttered under his breath and walked away.

"What's your name?" asked Libby, prying his hands free.

He looked up at her. "Jimmy."

"Jimmy what?"

"Just Jimmy."

She walked along the crowded aisle and thought about the little kids who knew their names, addresses, and phone numbers by the time they were four years old. Why hadn't anyone taught Jimmy these things?

Finally she stopped at the booth and told the woman at the window that Jimmy was lost and wanted his dad.

Before the woman could say anything a man who looked like a high school boy hurried up. "Jimmy! I've been looking all over for you!" He caught up the boy and hugged him tightly.

"Dad! Where were you? I could've been lost!"

Libby turned to walk away, then turned back with a smile when the man said thank you and Jimmy called good-bye. She said good-bye and hurried toward Penney's once again.

Just as she was passing the Martin Street exit someone grabbed her arm in a painful grip. She stared up at the stranger who had tried to take her to Mother. Her heart dropped to her feet and her eyes widened in terror.

"This time you won't get away!" the man said gruffly. His mustache moved up and down as he talked. His fake leather jacket had a cigarette burn on the sleeve.

"Let me go!" Libby struggled, but couldn't get away.

"Your mother wants you now!" The man locked his arm around her and pressed his hand over her mouth. "I don't want no noise from you. You belong with your mother and that's where you're going!"

Libby fought for breath as the man's hand slipped and pressed against her nose. If she could just open her mouth a little, she'd bite him and he'd let her go; then she'd run to Vera. Where was that policeman now? Had he left already? Didn't anyone notice what was happening to her?

The man shouldered open the door and cold air hit Libby's face. Oh, why had she helped Jimmy? Right now she'd be with Vera in Penney's, telling her about Tammy.

Libby's eyes widened. Tammy! Tammy would think Vera didn't want her and she'd leave. Maybe Tammy would hunt for Vera and talk to her. Libby struggled helplessly. What would Vera think when she didn't show up?

Finally the man reached his car and shoved her into the back seat. "If you make any move to get away, or scream, I'll knock you out. I'm tired of hearing your mother whine about wanting you home. You are going to her and you'll never run away again!"

Libby cowered in the farthest corner, her heart racing wildly. Could she open the passenger door and jump out at the stop sign ahead?

"If it were up to me, I'd say good riddance to you." The man glanced back, then ahead. He slowed to give way to a car driving on the main track, then pulled into the outside lane of the street. A car honked and he swore at it.

"Please, let me out!" Libby leaned forward. "I want to go home!"

"You're going home. Close your mouth and sit back. I don't want to get in no accident." He threaded his way through traffic, then turned off the main street and soon drove to a residential area.

Libby's mind whirled. Where did Mother live now? Would Chuck know how to find Mother when he realized Libby was missing?

Finally the man stopped the car in front of a run-down duplex. "I hope she's satisfied now that you're back," he muttered as he opened the door. He reached back for her, then angrily grabbed her when she backed away.

Her leg bumped the back of the seat and she caught back a cry of pain. She wanted to jerk away from him, but his grip was too tight. She hated the smell of beer on his breath as he turned to tell her to get a move on.

A garbage bag lay on a pile of dirty snow near the back door. A dog barked from down the block.

"Somebody help me!" she shouted loudly as he opened the back door.

He turned on her and slapped her hard across the

face. Tears filled her eyes as she covered the painful spot on her cheek. She was Elizabeth Gail Johnson, but he was treating her like Mother had treated plain Libby Dobbs. Would she be Mother's prisoner from now on?

"You think you're some hot-shot, don't you? You'll see how wrong you are!" He opened a door and pushed her inside.

She stumbled, then caught herself on the railing before she fell down the wooden steps that led to the basement. She turned but the door was slammed in her face. She heard the click of a lock and a sick feeling rose inside her, bringing a bitter taste to her mouth. She grabbed the knob, but it wouldn't turn. She was locked in! She slipped to the floor, her face pressed against the door. Was this really a nightmare? Or was she home with Mother, locked in again?

TEN
Prisoner

Libby looked around the messy basement, blinking hard to get rid of the tears. This was a time of action, and not a time to cry. The windows were too tiny and too close to the ceiling. She'd never be able to crawl out of them. Was there any way of escape?

She stopped, her hands clasped together. She took deep breaths to calm herself down. How could she have forgotten that her heavenly Father was with her to give her strength and help? Why hadn't she thought of that before?

"Heavenly Father, send someone to set me free. I want to go back to the Johnsons. Help me to get there."

Libby prayed for a while, then slowly walked around the small basement. Several boxes were stacked here and there. Two rakes stood in the corner next to a work bench.

A door slammed above and she tensed, her head up, her heart racing. Was Mother home? Would she walk downstairs and say, "Well, Libby. I finally have you where you belong. You'll never go back to that terrible family again. You are staying with me forever."

A chair scraped across the floor. A dust particle fell down and landed in Libby's eye. She blinked and rubbed her eye impatiently. Her eye watered and blurred her vision just as the door opened at the top of the stairs. Libby backed away so that she wouldn't have to see more than Mother's feet. Libby knew Mother couldn't see her except maybe her feet, too.

"So, the runaway finally came home. Jacob said he found you at the mall. Come up now and have some lunch."

Libby stumbled back even further so that she was completely out of sight. She would not go upstairs and see Mother! "You can't keep me here! I'll get out!"

Mother laughed dryly. "You're a very stubborn girl. I'm leaving the door unlocked so you can join me and Jacob. You'll get hungry and tired and you'll want out of that chilly basement before long."

The door slammed but the lock didn't click. Slowly Libby walked to the foot of the stairs and looked up at the closed door. The stairs seemed very dark and closed in. Libby shivered and wrapped her arms around herself. Fear pressed in on her as she remembered the time Mother had locked her in the closet and left her until Miss Miller came along and found her and let her out.

Why didn't Mother leave her alone and let her be happy at the Johnsons? What did Mother want out of her this time? Maybe she thought Chuck would pay to get her back.

Finally Libby crept up the steps, her heart racing so loud that she thought Mother and Jacob would hear. A cobweb caught on her cheek and she quickly rubbed it away, wrinkling her nose. She stopped at the door, listening intently. She couldn't hear anything on the other side. Slowly she turned the knob, then waited, her heart in her mouth. What if she pushed open the door and found Mother waiting to beat her? She forced herself to stay there and not run back down to the basement and hide.

She peeked into the kitchen. She saw a round table and three chairs and the counter. She waited, barely breathing. She heard voices from another room. Could she get out and run away? She caught her bottom lip between her teeth and stepped cautiously into the kitchen. Dirty dishes were stacked in the sink. An apartment size electric stove stood beside a white refrigerator. The sight of a telephone hanging on the wall next to the refrigerator sent Libby's heart leaping. She would call Chuck and he'd come get her! Her jacket suddenly felt hot. Perspiration pricked her skin and she twisted her neck uncomfortably. She'd better just get away and quickly! She would call Chuck from another phone.

She hastily grabbed the doorknob and tried to turn it. It wouldn't budge! Frantically she tried again. Shivers ran down her back. She looked at the knob and saw that it was the kind that could be opened only by a key. She was locked in! She bit her lip to keep from crying out, then slowly crept across the room to the phone. Would they be able to hear her dial from the other room?

The dial tone sounded loud, but her heart seemed even louder as she pressed the receiver to her ear. She dialed the number, expecting any minute to have Mother or Jacob jump out at her.

She held her breath as the phone rang. She could

picture Susan near the study phone or Ben in the family room near that phone. Vera was probably still at the mall looking for her. Had Vera called the police yet to report her missing?

"Who do you think you're calling?"

Libby jumped and the phone dropped from her hand to dangle almost to the floor. She backed away from Jacob, but he stood in the doorway, his arms crossed. "Let me go. Please! I don't want to stay here!"

He frowned as he studied her. "Your hair looks different. Or is it something else?" He shrugged. "No matter. Sit down and eat some lunch, then wash those dishes." He dropped the receiver in place on the phone.

"I want to go home," she whispered in agony. "Let me go home."

"You are home." He stepped toward her and she backed against the counter next to the sink. "Your mother is taking a nap. I said I'd take care of you. Eat a sandwich and clean up this kitchen."

She knotted and unknotted her fists. She glanced at the phone, then quickly away.

Jacob chuckled and shook his head. His dark hair looked as if he hadn't washed it for several days. "Don't get no ideas about calling for help from anybody. Who would want to help you?"

Her throat closed and she couldn't speak. Didn't he know that the Johnson family would help her? Didn't he know about all the friends that she'd made since she'd lived with the Johnsons?

Jacob turned and walked away. She heard him sink down on the couch, then prop his feet on a table. She peeked through the door and he was sitting with his head back and his eyes closed. Did he have the key to unlock the door?

Libby looked helplessly around the kitchen. She peered closely at the window in back of the table. Could she open it and jump out? She carefully unlocked it, then tried to push it up. Her arms ached from trying and she finally had to give up. She looked closer and saw that it was painted shut. She wanted to fling a chair through it and force her way out, but she knew Jacob would be on her before she could get away. She turned away as tears stung her eyes. She'd have to wait for an opportunity to run. They couldn't keep the door locked forever, and once it was open she'd be gone! She looked up to find Jacob watching her once again.

"Get on them dishes. I told your mother they'd be done by the time she got up from her nap." Jacob rubbed the back of his hand across his mouth, then rubbed his mustache carefully in place with his first two fingers.

Reluctantly Libby turned to the sink, then turned back. "Why can't I load them in the dishwasher?"

"Don't get smart. You know it's broke. Now, get to work."

She lifted her thin shoulders and let them fall. "How should I know it's broken?"

"Ha ha. Very funny. Get to work!" He frowned and his dark brows almost met over his hooked nose. "Take off your coat and wash them dishes now!"

She folded her arms across her chest and shook her head. Somehow the thought of taking off her jacket made staying too permanent.

Just then someone knocked on the door. Libby froze, her eyes riveted to the door. Was it Chuck? Oh, how could it be? He had no idea where she was.

Jacob peered out the window, then frowned impatiently. "Not that woman again," he muttered. He turned to Libby. "You get down in the basement again until she leaves."

Libby lifted her chin, daring him to make her, but he grabbed her and shoved her. "If you cause any trouble, you'll be sorry," he whispered close to her ear so that she could smell his bad breath.

She stumbled and caught herself with the railing, then stood there helplessly as he closed and locked the basement door. She pressed her ear to the door and heard him greet the visitor.

"Where's my sister?" Libby heard the woman ask sharply.

"Phyllis LaDere!" whispered Libby, her eyes wide. Should she bang on the door and tell Phyllis what was happening?

Would Phyllis even care? She'd probably say to keep Libby locked up forever.

"I want you to wake her up right now. I want to talk to her. I want to talk to Tammy to see if she saw Libby like she said she would."

Libby frowned in confusion. What did Phyllis mean?

"You can't talk to Tammy. Why don't you go home and leave us be. We can't help you with your daughter."

"You mean you won't!"

"Same difference."

The door opened, then slammed, then the lock clicked sharply against Libby's ear. She backed down the stairs and waited for Jacob to open the door and demand that she come up. She waited, listening, then slowly turned the knob and opened the door. The kitchen was empty. Maybe the outside door was unlocked. It just had to be!

Libby's mouth felt bone-dry, as she tried the knob. It wouldn't turn and she wanted to beat against the door and scream and yell, but she stood quietly, her head down, her shoulders drooping.

A hand grabbed her roughly and spun her around. Jacob's face was dark with anger.

"You will not get away again, girl. I won't go off looking the countryside over for you. If you know what's good for you, you'll wash them dishes and settle in here nice and proper."

"Jacob, what's all the yelling?"

Libby clung to the back of a chair to keep from falling at the sound of Mother's voice. Libby heard footsteps coming and she looked wildly around for a way to escape. Jacob was blocking the door to the front room and the outside door was locked. She was trapped!

"Just go lay back down, Sugar. I'm taking care of things just fine out here."

Mother brushed past Jacob, then stood staring at Libby. "Libby!" The woman turned to Jacob. "You fool! This is Libby, not Tammy!"

Libby could not believe her eyes or her ears. This was not Mother! This was Phyllis LaDere!

"Libby?" asked Jacob dumbfoundedly. "Are you sure?"

"I should know my own daughter," said Phyllis sharply. "I sent you after Tammy and you bring back Libby!"

"What are we going to do now?" asked Jacob, spreading his hands.

"*We* are not going to do anything. *You* are!"

Libby licked her lips. "Just let me go and I'll go home."

"Sure you will," said Phyllis, with a sneer. "You won't

cause a bit of trouble for me. You'll go home and tell that rich family of yours that you went for a long walk. I bet!" She turned to Jacob. "You made this mess, now fix it!"

"I want to go home!" Libby lifted her chin high. "You must let me go!"

"Must we?" Phyllis chuckled dryly. "Must we?"

"I thought there was something funny about Tammy," said Jacob, shaking his head. "And here it wasn't Tammy at all. Has anyone ever told you how much you look like Tammy?" Libby glared at him and he laughed.

Phyllis pushed back her bleached blonde hair and walked out of the room.

Jacob caught Libby's arm and twisted it around her back. "Tammy's not here and you are. You get that coat off and get them dishes done. I'll think about what to do with you later." He released her and stepped back.

Slowly she unzipped her jacket and slipped it off. Her arm hurt but she wouldn't let herself wince. She hung the jacket on the back of the chair next to the door and walked to the sinkful of dishes. Would she ever see the Johnsons again?

ELEVEN
The call

Libby picked up her watch from the counter and slipped it back on. She frowned. She'd been washing dishes for an hour. She'd been gone from the mall over two hours. What did Vera think happened to her? Oh, she had to get away!

She tiptoed across the kitchen and peeked into the front room. Jacob lay snoring on the couch, one arm across his eyes and the other on his chest.

Quick as a flash Libby was at the telephone dialing Chuck's store. She waited barely breathing as it rang four times and then Chuck answered. Libby felt almost too weak to talk.

"Dad, it's me, Libby," she whispered as loud as she dared. She kept looking toward the front room for signs of Jacob.

"Elizabeth! We've been frantic! The police are looking for you. Where are you?"

"A man grabbed me and I'm at Phyllis LaDere's house. They won't let me go!" She knew she was talking too loud, but she couldn't help it. In a minute she would be crying hysterically and she couldn't allow that.

"Tell me the address and I'll come get you."

"I don't know it, Dad!"

"Give me the phone number and I'll get the address." He sounded grim and she knew he would be after her shortly.

Before she could read the number Jacob pressed the receiver in place and roughly shoved her away from the phone.

"What do you think you're doing? You'll be sorry you did that, girl!" He stepped toward her, his face dark with anger, his fists doubled at his sides. She wanted to run, but she stood ready for him.

She kicked him in the shin and he yelped and grabbed his leg. She doubled her fist and punched him in the face. Blood spurted from his nose.

He grabbed her and she screamed, kicking and squirming. Her skin crawled at his touch. "Let me go!"

"Let her go!" Phyllis's voice rang out and Jacob dropped his hands and backed away.

Libby stumbled and caught herself on the edge of the table. She stared at Phyllis who stood with her hands on her waist. Her dusty rose robe almost touched the floor and was tied around the waist with a wide belt. She was glaring at Jacob as he held a hanky to his nose.

"Are you trying to get us in more trouble than we are already?" Phyllis asked as she walked across the kitchen in her bare feet. Her nails were painted red and part of the polish was chipped off the big toe on her left foot. She tore off a paper towel and held it under the cold water. She squeezed it out and handed it to Jacob, then she turned to Libby. "I almost forgot the way you

can fight. Tammy never learned to do that. Do you
know where Tammy is?"

Libby swallowed hard. Should she tell about talking
to Tammy in the mall?

"Well? Have you seen Tammy today?" Libby nodded.

"Where?" Phyllis stepped closer and Libby smelled
her breath mint.

"In the mall."

Jacob nodded. "I saw her go into the mall, and then
when I saw Libby I just thought she was Tammy."

"Did you talk to her?" Phyllis fingered her belt.

Libby nodded again and dropped to a chair. She
watched warily as Phyllis sat down across from her.
Finally Jacob pulled out the third chair and sat down, too.

"Why is she so determined to run away from me?"
Phyllis sounded as if she'd burst into tears and Jacob
caught her hand and held it. She smiled wanly at him,
then turned back to Libby. "What did she say to you?"

Libby locked her fingers together in her lap. She dare
not tell what Tammy had said. "We just talked."

"Is she coming home?"

"She said she wanted to." She *had* said that! She'd
said she wanted to pick up her special things.

Phyllis leaned back with a sigh, "We fight a lot, but I
want her to stay with me. I will not lose my daughter
the way Marie lost you."

Libby flushed and looked down at the table. A small
scratch marred the formica top. She had to get away!
Where was Chuck? Was he right this minute speeding
to rescue her? Her heart leaped and she wanted to jump
up and grab her jacket to be ready for him. But how
could he find her when she hadn't been able to give him
the address or phone number?

Just then a key grated in the lock and Libby looked at Phyllis who was staring open-mouthed at the door.

"It has to be Tammy," she whispered, slowly standing up.

Libby jumped up, her eyes wide. Tammy would help her! Tammy would set her free! Libby grabbed her jacket and slipped it on as the door opened wide and Tammy walked in. She stopped and stared at Libby in surprise, then anger.

"It's about time you showed up," said Phyllis sharply. "I've been looking for you for days. Where have you been?"

Tammy glanced at her mother, then back to Libby. "I waited for over an hour!"

"Jacob brought me here," said Libby barely above a whisper. "Help me get away."

"Help you?" Tammy shrugged. "Why should I? I was desperate and you sure didn't help me."

"What are you talking about?" asked Phyllis as she caught Tammy's arm and shook her. "Why were you desperate?"

Tammy jerked free. "To get away from you! Do you think I want this kind of life?" She pointed at Jacob. "Do you know that he tried to pay some guy to take me out?"

Jacob flushed as Phyllis turned on him. "Is that true?"

"We needed some money, Phylly. What could I do?"

She swore at him and Libby cringed. Tammy stood beside Libby and studied her thoughtfully.

"You have no business talking to me that way," said Jacob gruffly. "I've been taking good care of you and you know it."

Phyllis squared her shoulders. "Not any longer. Get out right now and never come near me or Tammy again!"

Jacob laughed and shook his head. "Sure, I'll do that. I'll leave you to deal with that rich family Libby lives with."

Libby's stomach tightened sickeningly. Did Jacob know that she'd completed the phone call to Chuck?

"What do you mean?" Phyllis grabbed his arms and tried to shake him, but he was too big.

"She made a call before I could stop her. She told them where she was."

"Why didn't you tell me?" Phyllis's eyes looked wild. "I'll get packed and we'll leave now!" She rushed away, then looked over her shoulder at Tammy. "Pack your things. Be ready in ten minutes or sooner."

"Wait." Jacob hurried after Phyllis, begging her to take him with her.

Libby turned to Tammy. "Unlock the door and let me out."

"Why should I help you?" Tammy pushed back her jacket and stood with her hands on her hips. "I needed help and you didn't help me."

Libby wanted to scream. "I planned on helping you. I would have taken you home with me, but Jacob grabbed me and forced me to his car. He thought I was you."

"Is this the truth, Libby?"

"Why would I lie?"

"To get me to help you."

"Oh, Tammy!" Libby grabbed for the door. "Open it for me! I must get away. Don't leave me alone with Jacob!"

"Can I go with you?" asked Tammy barely above a whisper.

Libby nodded. "But we have to hurry."

Tammy pulled out her key, then dropped it.

Libby scrambled for it and could barely hold it in her icy fingers. Cold chills ran up and down her back. Her hand trembled so much that she couldn't get the key into the lock. Tammy jerked it from her and inserted it. She turned it and Libby bit back a shout of victory.

"Where do you think you girls are going?" asked Jacob as he reached around them and slammed the door again. He turned the key and pocketed it. Libby leaped on him, beating his chest with her fists.

"Help me, Tammy!" she shouted. "Get the key from him!"

Jacob caught Libby and jerked her arms behind her. "You are a wildcat. But I can handle you all right." He chuckled. "I'll have fun taking care of you."

Phyllis rushed in. "Tammy, let's go!"

"I'm not ready."

"What?" shrieked Phyllis, awkwardly carrying her suitcases. "You will have to leave your things. We don't want to be here when Chuck Johnson gets here with the police."

"I'm staying with Libby." Tammy stuck out her jaw stubbornly.

"Oh, no, you're not!" Phyllis dropped a case and caught Tammy's arm tightly. You are going with me and that's final!"

"You're hurting me!" Tammy struggled, but Phyllis wouldn't let her go.

Libby watched helplessly as Phyllis forced Tammy from the house. The door slammed. Libby heard Jacob's heart beating and smelled his beer breath. She had to get free!

A car started and drove away. Libby knew it was Phyllis and Tammy. "Why don't you let me go? I just want to get home where I belong."

Jacob released her with a chuckle. "Sure, you want to

tell the police all about me, don't you? I can't take that chance, girl. I don't want to go back to jail ever again, and I won't!"

Suddenly Libby leaped away from Jacob and ran into the front room. She saw a short hallway and ran to the next room and closed the door just as Jacob started in. He yelped in pain, then beat against the locked door. Her chest rose and fell as she leaned against the door, wildly looking for a way to escape.

"Unlock this door or I'll break it down!"

She knew he could do just that. Fearfully she rushed to the lone window and tried to open it. It was also painted shut. Dust puffed from the light blue curtains and Libby sneezed. Should she break the window and crawl through?

Jacob hit against the door, jarring it loudly. Libby jumped, her hand clamped over her mouth. The next lunge against the door would break it open. What should she do?

The distant sound of a siren sent her heart leaping. She raced to the door, then jumped back. If she walked out that door Jacob would grab her.

The siren was closer and Libby held her breath. Did Jacob think it was the police and Chuck coming to get her? It just had to be!

Suddenly the siren sounded very loud and Libby knew the police car was just outside. But it didn't stop and soon the sound died away in the distance.

"No," whispered Libby in agony, her eyes closed and her fists doubled at her sides. "Oh, no, no, no."

Weakly she sank to the edge of the bed, shivering violently. She was still Jacob's prisoner. She stared at the door in fear. What would he do to her once he broke down the door and grabbed her?

The bed shook with her shivering and tears raced down her cheeks. What was she going to do now?

TWELVE
Mother

Finally Libby pushed herself off the bed and stood uncertainly. What was Jacob doing? He was very quiet. Was he just outside the door, waiting for her to step out so he could grab her? She swallowed hard.

A dog barked outdoors and Libby jumped. Then carefully she tiptoed across the floor and pressed her ear to the door. Could she hear breathing? She frowned. It was her own ragged breathing she heard.

She licked her lips. "Jacob? Are you there?" she asked in a soft trembling voice. She waited, then called his name a little louder. Finally she turned the lock and pulled open the door, a crack at a time. Her hands were wet with perspiration and one at a time she rubbed them down her pants.

Cautiously she tiptoed into the hall, then peeked into the bathroom. It was empty. A car drove past, sounding loud in the silence. Why hadn't Chuck found her yet?

Libby looked over her shoulder at the open bedroom door. Maybe she should run in there and lock herself in until Chuck did find her. But what if that took hours? She had to get away!

Slowly she walked into the front room. Her heart drummed in her ears and perspiration popped out on her forehead. Where was Jacob?

She saw the phone on the kitchen wall and she rushed to it with a strangled sob. She'd call Chuck again, and he'd come get her and take her home where she'd be safe.

Suddenly a rough hand grabbed her. She screamed as she jerked around to find Jacob.

"I knew you'd come out," he said gruffly. "You'll pay for all the trouble you've caused me!" A muscle jumped in his cheek and his eyes were hard and angry. Libby wanted to scream and scream, but she knew he'd slap her if she did.

"I want to go home," she whispered brokenly. "Let me go. Please, let me go!"

He yanked her across the room and slammed her down on a chair. "Now sit there until I decide what we're going to do. We don't have much time."

Libby clasped the sides of her chair seat and forced herself to stop shivering. Jacob must not know how scared she was.

"Chuck Johnson will get you for this! He'll hunt you down until he finds you, and you'll be very sorry!"

Jacob pushed his face close to hers and his breath felt hot on her face. "Shut your mouth! If you open it again, I'll shut it for you." He turned and walked jerkily across the floor, then back. He frowned and tugged nervously at his mustache. "If I had a car I'd know just where to take you." He cracked his knuckles. "Phyllis shouldn't have left me. She knows I don't have a car."

Libby bit her tongue to keep from saying anything. Could Jacob hear the wild beating of her heart? Why wasn't she big and strong so she could jump on him and beat him and grab the key? Maybe she'd be Jacob's prisoner forever. She'd never become a famous concert pianist. She'd never be known as one of the Johnsons. How long would they search for her? Would they forget her? She ducked her head and fought against the tears stinging her eyes.

Just then someone pounded on the door. Libby leaped up and Jacob grabbed her, clamping his sweaty hand over her mouth. She struggled, her eyes almost popping out of her head. Was it Chuck?

The pounding continued as Jacob carefully peeked out the window. He chuckled dryly and released Libby. She stared at him in surprise. What was he up to this time?

He unlocked the door and swung it wide. Libby tensed, ready to spring out the opening, then stumbled back as Mother stepped in. Libby wanted to evaporate so Mother couldn't see her. Frantically she looked around for a way of escape. There was none.

"Hello, Libby," said Marie Dobbs, looking at Libby coldly.

Libby pressed her lips tightly closed as Mother pulled off her coat and draped it over the back of a chair. She tugged her blue sweater over her too-tight jeans, then folded her arms.

"Well, Libby."

"What are you doing here, Marie?" asked Jacob with a scowl. "Did Phyllis come see you?"

Marie shook her head, then pushed a stray piece of bleached blonde hair in place. "That no-good sister of mine don't tell me anything! I got a call from Chuck Johnson."

Libby's heart leaped. "Dad called? Did you tell him I was here?"

"Dad?" Marie laughed harshly. "Your dad is Frank Dobbs and he's dead."

Libby clenched her fists at her sides and lifted her chin high. "Chuck is my dad now. He adopted me!"

"What good will that adoption paper do if he can't find you?" Marie stepped toward Libby. "You're going to stay with me from now on. I should never have signed that paper. You're my kid, Libby, and you always will be. We'll leave the state for good, and no one will ever hear from us again."

Libby backed away until she pressed against the sink. How could this be happening to her? Was she asleep and dreaming this terrible nightmare?

"Are you forgetting about me, Marie?" asked Jacob as he leaned against the refrigerator. "I think we can help each other, don't you?"

Marie looked disdainfully at Jacob. "Why should I help you?"

He grinned and tugged at his mustache. "I'm bigger than you. I have your daughter and you can't take her unless I say so. Maybe I'll keep her with me. I might enjoy having a girl like her around."

Libby looked wildly toward the door. Her heart stopped. Jacob had left the key in the lock! She had to get to the door and get away!

"Why would you want Libby?" asked Marie sharply.

Jacob jangled the change in his pocket. "I could find some way for her to work for me." He laughed wickedly and Libby trembled.

"Well, Libby is going with me!" Marie stood with her hands on her waist. "If you need a place to stay for a while, Jacob, come with us. But don't expect to hang around very long."

Suddenly Libby rushed past Mother and reached the door. She fumbled with the key and finally turned it. She felt like she was moving in slow motion. Just as the door opened Jacob jerked Libby away from it. She stumbled back into Mother. Hot, angry tears filled Libby's eyes.

"Don't try that again, Libby." Mother's hands bit into Libby's arms. "You're going with me, and that's final!"

"No," whispered Libby, her head down. She could smell Mother's strong perfume and stale tobacco. Oh, she must get away from Mother!

"I'm taking you to my car and if you make any trouble I'll have Jacob handle it," said Marie Dobbs as she dragged Libby toward the door that Jacob held open for

them. Cold air blew against Libby. A dog barked and Libby wanted to scream for help. She knew if she tried, Jacob would cover her mouth or knock her out.

"I'll drive," said Jacob as he walked in the snow beside Libby.

Marie jerked open the car door with her free hand, then pushed Libby into the back seat. She fell into the seat, striking her head against the far side. Moaning, she sat up, her hand on her head. What was Mother going to do with her? Marie climbed into the back seat with Libby as Jacob started the engine.

Jacob drove down the quiet street and onto a busy crossroad. Marie kept a firm grip on Libby's arm.

"I've been waiting for this day, Libby. You'll never get away from me again."

Libby pressed against the seat as fear pricked her skin. "You don't want me. Let me go back to the Johnsons!"

"Never!" Marie spit the word out, then smiled slightly. "I'm your family, Libby. I'll take care of you the way I should have all these years. I'll buy your clothes and food and see that you get to school. Maybe we'll go West. I know your no-good dad left you a small bit of property in Nebraska. We can go there to stay and no one will bother us."

Libby couldn't speak around the hard lump in her throat.

Jacob said, "It would be dumb to go to Libby's place in Nebraska. It would be one of the first places the police would look." Jacob slowed and turned onto a narrow street lined with cars. "You'd better go to a large city and just get lost there. I know Chicago. We could go there."

Libby's heart sank. Chicago! How would she ever find her way home from there!

94

Suddenly Libby leaned toward the window. She recognized this part of town. She'd lived nearby with Bud and Sandy Black when she was eight. Did they still live in the same house? Would they even remember her if she could get to them for help?

"What are you so excited about, Libby?" asked Marie sharply. "Did you see someone you know?"

Libby kept looking out the window and wouldn't answer. She would never talk to Mother again as long as she lived!

Jacob pulled into a narrow drive and turned off the engine. "You are home, Libby," he said, grinning over his shoulder. "This is far from what you're used to at the Johnson's, but it'll be a roof over your head."

Libby glanced at the tiny house that badly needed paint. Once she was inside that house, would she ever get out again?

"Don't get any smart ideas about screaming for help when we get out of the car," said Marie. "Nobody around here cares how loud you scream. You won't get help from nobody!" Marie picked a blonde hair off her sleeve and dropped it away from her. "We're going to get out of the car and walk to the house." She turned to Jacob. "My house key is on the key ring. You go first and unlock the front door; then we'll come in. I don't trust this girl of mine."

"I'm not your girl!" cried Libby. "I belong to the Johnsons!"

Marie laughed and shook her head. "Not any longer. You might as well get used to living with me. Who knows? We might get to liking each other."

Jacob laughed as he opened the car door. Cold air rushed in before he slammed it shut. Several boys ran past, shouting noisily. A car without a muffler roared past. Libby looked frantically around for help.

She remembered that Chuck had told her often that God was always with her and would help her. Silently she cried out to God for help as Jacob motioned for them to come to the house.

Marie opened the door, then stood beside the car as she tilted the back seat for Libby. "You'll have to learn to like living with me, Libby. I won't stand for that long face and those sad eyes."

Libby stumbled out and Marie caught her arm in a tight grip, then pushed the car door closed.

"Welcome home, Libby." Marie chuckled and Libby felt sick to her stomach.

Marie stumbled on a clump of snow and her hold loosened. Libby jerked, then shoved against Marie. Marie stumbled back and plopped onto a snow bank. Libby raced away with Marie screaming for Jacob to catch her. Could Jacob run fast enough to catch her? Oh, she had to get away!

Running faster, Libby tried to listen for Jacob behind her. All she could hear were her pounding feet and heart.

She ran around a little girl on a trike, then cut across a yard. She recognized the alley where she'd once played years ago. She ran faster. A pain shot through her side and her throat was sore from breathing the cold air.

What if Jacob followed her in Mother's car? Oh, that couldn't happen, could it? She had to keep away from the streets and alley.

She heard brakes screech and she looked over her shoulder. Jacob had found her! Oh, what would happen to her now?

THIRTEEN
Escape

Libby froze in fear at the sight of Jacob running across the yard toward her. She wanted to just stand still and scream and scream. Finally she turned and raced to the fence and scrambled over it into another yard. Someone yelled at her, but she kept running. The pain in her side almost doubled her over.

She reached a sidewalk and ran down it, her shoes slapping loudly. Was Jacob right behind her? Dare she look back? She swerved onto another lawn, then leaped another fence. Her chest rose and fell and her mouth hung open as she gulped for air. Wildly she looked around for a place to hide. She saw a tree with a rope ladder and looked up to find a tree house. Her heart leaped. She would hide in the tree house and neither Jacob nor Mother would ever find her.

Frantically she clutched the rope ladder and scrambled up. She plopped on the floor of the tree house, panting for breath. Finally she tugged the ladder up and laid it in a heap beside her. Was she safe at last? Did her red and white jacket show against the winter gray of the tree? She moved slightly and bumped into a can of nails. A hammer lay beside the can. She could see where new boards were added on the sides of the wooden platform. What if the person building the tree house were to come out to work on it now? She shivered and slid lower, her heart racing painfully.

Noises of the neighborhood seemed far away and unreal to her as she waited impatiently in the tree house. How long would Jacob search before he gave up and went back to report to Mother?

Libby covered her face with ice hands. Just this morning she'd had a piano lesson with Rachael Avery, then gone shopping with Vera at the mall. Was Vera still frantically looking for her? Vera had probably gone home to be with Ben and Susan and Kevin and Toby. Were they worried about her? Would she ever see them again?

Tears filled her eyes and she quickly wiped them away. She didn't have time to cry!

Slowly she peered over the edge of the tree house. Her legs and back felt stiff and sore. She groaned and frowned, then looked all around the yard below and the yard next door. They looked deserted. She couldn't see the children she heard shouting and laughing. A dog barked and she couldn't see it either. Traffic noises seemed close and she painfully dragged herself to the other side of the tree house to look. Cars zoomed along with a few pickups and a diesel truck. A police car passed the truck and Libby wanted to shout for help. She bit her lower lip and groaned in frustration.

Once again she looked in the yard under the tree house, then slowly lowered the rope ladder. Very carefully she turned and climbed down until her feet touched the ground; then she was off and running toward the busy highway. She remembered a phone at the corner. She fumbled in her pocket and almost tripped. At least she had change to make a call.

Several minutes later Libby breathlessly lifted the telephone receiver and dropped in her change. She looked nervously around, then pressed the police emergency number listed next to the phone. Her hand shook and she almost dropped the receiver. When someone answered, tears of relief filled her eyes.

"This is Libby . . . Johnson, and I need help." Her voice sounded high and unreal and she cleared her throat before she answered the many questions.

Once she heard a car slow beside her and she looked around in panic, but the car drove on. What *if* Mother or Jacob drove this way and found her before the police finished talking to her and came for her? Oh, that was too terrible to think about!

Later she looked around for a place to hide until the police car came for her. Maybe she could stay near the filling station at the corner. She shook her head. She had to stay beside the phone so she wouldn't miss the patrol car. Her legs felt like melting marshmallows. Her stomach was in a cold, hard knot. She whimpered in fear, then looked quickly around to make sure no one had heard her. But no one was around to hear her.

A car stopped and she whirled around, then cried out as Chuck hurried toward her. She ran to him and flung her arms around his neck. Oh, he felt good!

"Tell me what happened, Elizabeth," he said with his arms tightly around her. "I heard the police call come in about you and I hurried right down."

She burst into tears and he let her cry for a while,

then held her away. She sniffed hard as she looked in his dear face. She could not live without him! She tried to speak, but no sound came.

"Officer Barns is waiting in his car to talk to you, Elizabeth. I'll give you a few minutes, then let's get home. I had them call Vera at home to let her know you had been found, but I want to call her to tell her you're with me and safe."

Libby saw Officer Barns standing beside his car; then she pressed her face against Chuck's shoulder while he called Vera.

"Tell Vera that you're all right, Elizabeth," said Chuck in a low voice as he held out the receiver.

"Mom?"

"Oh, Libby!"

Libby burst into tears again. "Mom, I'm all right. We'll be home soon."

Chuck held her tightly as he talked a minute longer with Vera. He hung up and walked Libby to the waiting officer.

His car was warm and smelled of chocolate. Libby's stomach cramped with hunger and she realized she hadn't eaten since breakfast and it was almost supper-time.

With Chuck beside her, she told what had happened to her.

"Show us where your mother lives, please," said Officer Barns grimly. "I want to talk to her."

Libby shivered and gripped Chuck's large hand tighter. "I don't want to see her! I can't!" She turned to Chuck, her eyes large. "Please, don't make me see her. She was going to take me away and never let me live with you!"

100

Chuck patted her cheek. "You won't have to see your mother. But we must know where she lives so Officer Barns can handle this. Just show us the house and we'll take care of it from there."

"I will," Libby said barely above a whisper.

"What way from here?" asked the officer as he started his car.

Several minutes later Libby pointed to the tiny house,

then waited with Chuck while the officer went to the door. He came back later, shaking his head.

"It's empty. They've already left and they've probably left town. But we'll find them. They can't have gotten far."

Libby leaned back in relief. She reluctantly showed them where Phyllis LaDere lived, but that house was empty also, so they drove to Chuck's car.

"Now can we go home, Dad?" she whispered tiredly.

He nodded and thanked Officer Barns. "If there's anything I can do to help, let me know. We'll expect to hear from you," said Chuck as he stood beside the police car. He looked tired as he said good-bye and led Libby to the car.

She sat inside, feeling warm and cared for even though the car was cold. She sighed and hugged herself tightly. Soon she'd be home where she belonged. She leaned toward Chuck as he waited a minute before pulling into traffic.

"I love you, Dad. Thank you for finding me today."

He winked at her. "I knew we'd find you, Elizabeth. But, I must admit, it took longer than I liked."

"Were you scared?" she asked in surprise.

He nodded.

"So was I! But I'm not scared now. I'm hungry." Libby laughed.

Chuck squeezed her hand. "We'll get home and have supper with the family." He pulled into the street and drove quickly away.

Family! She'd wondered if she'd ever see her new family again, but soon she would. She thought about Tammy and there was a lump in her throat. What would become of Tammy?

"Dad, I wish we could help Tammy."

"I do, too, Elizabeth." Chuck slowed and turned onto Crane Street. "And we will the first chance we get. We'll pray for her, too. God loves her as much as he loves us. He wants her to be happy also."

Libby nodded, then sat back and closed her eyes. Someday Tammy would find a loving family to live with. Someday Tammy would be happy.

FOURTEEN
Home again

With Chuck behind her, Libby stood in the family room doorway, quietly watching Vera, Susan, and the boys. Vera sat in her chair with her head back, her eyes closed, and her cross-stitched picture in her lap. The others were watching TV.

"Hi," said Libby.

Vera leaped up and rushed to Libby. She hugged Libby close, then held her back and looked at her, then hugged her again. "Oh, Libby, Libby. This has been the longest day of my life!"

"She's safe now," said Chuck. "She's home where she belongs."

"Tell us what happened, Libby," said Susan, bouncing up and down until her red-gold hair jumped too.

"Were you kidnapped?" asked Kevin, punching his glasses against his round face.

"How did you get away?" asked Toby, tugging at Libby's hand. His freckles stood out boldly. "Did they hurt you?"

"Let Libby talk," said Ben impatiently.

Libby tipped back her head and laughed. Oh, it was good to be home! She looked at her family. "I'll tell you everything, starting with the first phone call before my birthday."

"And I thought that call had been a prank!" said Ben, slapping his forehead.

Libby shook her head. "It was my real cousin Tammy LaDere. She needed my help." Libby sat down and watched the others as they made themselves comfortable around the room.

After a long time, Libby finally finished her story. Everyone was quiet; then Susan leaped up, her blue eyes bright.

"I'll have to call Joe and tell him you're home safe."

"Don't talk long," said Vera. "There are others who want to know also." She turned to Libby as Susan hurried from the room. "Brian Parr offered to go look for you, but we had no idea where to look, so he said to call if we heard anything. And Jill called at least a dozen times. I said you'd call her."

Libby rubbed her hand down her jeans. Maybe Jill wanted to be best friends again. Libby smiled. She wanted to be best friends with Jill again. If Jill wanted to love Adam, she could.

Susan rushed back in, saying she was off the phone. Her cheeks were flushed. "Joe said to tell you that he's glad you're home safely. He said he'd see you in church tomorrow." Susan took a deep breath, smiled and sort of drifted down onto the couch.

"I'll see Joe tomorrow, too," said Kevin breathlessly as he took a deep breath and clutched his heart dramatically.

Everyone laughed. The phone rang and Libby

jumped, then laughed self-consciously as Vera answered it. She talked a few minutes, hung up, and turned to Libby. "Jill is coming to see you now. She said it's very important and she can't wait."

Libby nodded. She wanted to see Jill, too.

"I'll get supper and make a few phone calls from the kitchen," said Vera from the doorway. "Who wants to help me?" She crooked her finger at Chuck and motioned for him to join her.

He jumped up. "I volunteer to help with supper. Boys, start the chores, please."

"I'll help them," said Susan.

Libby jumped up. "I'll do my chores right after Jill leaves."

Chuck slipped his arm around her. "Not tonight, Elizabeth. Why don't you rest quietly before supper and wait for Jill? You've had quite a day."

Several minutes later there was a knock on Libby's bedroom door and Jill walked in.

Jill stood in the middle of the room and looked as if she'd burst into tears. "Libby, please forgive me for being mean to you. After I found out you were missing I almost went crazy. I want you for my best friend and if you want me to forget about Adam, I will."

Libby laughed softly. "No, Jill. You can love anyone you want. I'm sure sorry about the misunderstanding. You see, it was Tammy who was talking with Adam, and not me at all. Tammy and I look alike, but we don't act alike. She loves boys!" Libby rolled her eyes. "Adam is only a friend, nothing more. You don't have to be jealous."

Jill sat on the big round hassock with her arms folded across herself. "It sure hurts to be in love, Libby. I wish I was old so I wouldn't have to think about boyfriends."

Libby laughed, glad to be here with Jill even if she could only talk about love and Adam.

Jill took a deep breath, then let it out. "Tell me about this terrible day, Libby. I want to know everything. Maybe I could write a book about it. Were you scared? What did you think about? Does Tammy really look like you?"

Libby picked Pinky off her bed, then sat cross-legged in the middle of her bed with Pinky held tightly in her arms. "It all started with that phone call that I got before my birthday." This time she knew she had Jill's full attention, and it felt good.

Later after her shower Libby walked downstairs in her robe and slippers to the family room. For some reason she felt too restless to sleep. Piano music drifted from the family room and she knew Vera was practicing the piece she was to play in church in the morning.

Libby stood quietly in the darkened hallway and listened contentedly. She jumped when someone spoke to her. She turned to find Chuck standing in his study doorway. The light from the study beamed into the hall, making a path.

"Want to talk a while, honey?" he asked.

Slowly she walked to his study and sat down. Chuck sat next to her on the leather couch and put his arm around her.

"Couldn't you sleep, Elizabeth?"

She shook her head. "I can't quit thinking about this day. If I close my eyes I'm afraid I'll be locked in with Jacob or Mother or Phyllis LaDere again."

Taking one of her hands in his, Chuck said, "The bad experience is over, Elizabeth. The only way you can put it out of your mind is to pray for them. Jesus said to pray for your enemies. Pray for them, Elizabeth, and forgive them. Then, and only then, will you be able to release the fear inside you and the bad feelings toward them. Once you do that, you'll be able to sleep and continue your life happily."

Libby hesitated as she stared at the tips of her pink slippers. Finally she looked up at Chuck. "I'll pray for them, but it won't be easy to forgive them!"

"Just obey what God's Word says, easy or hard. You must answer for yourself only, not for the others."

Libby nodded, then asked Chuck if he would pray with her.

Later as she stood to leave, the phone rang. She locked her hands together and her heart raced as Chuck answered it. He hesitated, then handed it to her.

"It's Tammy LaDere," he said softly.

Libby gulped, then hurried to take the receiver, "Hello, Tammy."

"I'm glad you're home, Libby. I kept thinking about you. I finally got away from Mother long enough to call. I hope Jacob didn't hurt you."

"He didn't." Libby didn't want to tell Tammy the whole story, so she waited quietly.

"Libby, I have to stay with Mother right now, but just as soon as I can I'm going to find a family like yours." She paused. "Would your family adopt me, too?"

"I don't know, but I do know they would help you, Tammy."

"Thank you, Libby." Tammy's words dissolved in a sob. She sniffed loudly. "I'll talk to you again first chance I can, and I'll write to you."

"I'll pray for you, Tammy."

"Thanks."

Libby heard the soft click of the receiver, then the dial tone. Slowly she replaced the receiver and looked at Chuck. "I want her to be happy, Dad."

"I know you do, Elizabeth."

She kissed his cheek, said good night, and slowly walked back upstairs. She stood inside her bedroom and looked around at all that belonged to her. Finally she smiled. This wonderful miracle had happened to her. Someday it would happen for Tammy, too.

If you've enjoyed the Elizabeth Gail series, be sure to read the adventures of Teddy Jo!

The Teddy Jo adventures are available at your local bookstore, or you may order by mail (U.S. and territories only). Send your check or money order plus $1.25 per book ordered for postage and handling to:

Tyndale D.M.S., Box 80, Wheaton, IL 60189

Prices subject to change. Allow 4-6 weeks for delivery.

Tyndale House Publishers, Inc.